DIRTY ALLIANCE

SPECIAL WEAPONS & TACTICS 4

PEYTON BANKS

CONTENTS

Chapter 1   1

Chapter 2   17

Chapter 3   28

Chapter 4   40

Chapter 5   50

Chapter 6   64

Chapter 7   76

Chapter 8   89

Chapter 9   103

Chapter 10   112

Chapter 11   125

Chapter 12   136

Chapter 13   148

Chapter 14   159

Chapter 15   172

Chapter 16   183

Chapter 17   197

Chapter 18   211

Chapter 19   222

Chapter 20   235

Chapter 21   245

Chapter 22   256

Chapter 23   271

Epilogue   280

A Note From the Author   289

Dallas (Trust & Honor 1)   290

About the Author   301

Also by Peyton Banks   303

1

"Give us your money," a voice demanded.

Myles froze in place. He stared at the ATM in disbelief. It was a little before seven in the morning, and he was about to get robbed while taking money out.

Who goes out to rob people this early?

"I don't think you want to do this," he murmured. A deep breath escaped him as he drew his hand back from the machine.

"But we do. How much did you take out?" another voice asked.

"A hundred." Something hard pressed into Myles's shoulder.

The barrel of a gun.

His muscles grew tense. He wasn't sure about the men standing behind him, but Myles was highly trained in the deadliest of combat. With Myles having served his country, Uncle Sam ensured he was an elite soldier.

"That will be a start. Go ahead and put your card back in and take out the max, old man," the first voice said with a sarcastic chuckle. "We'll even let you live."

He bit back a growl.

Fuck this.

They ran up on the wrong *old man* today.

He stood to his full height and turned around. He glared at the two young punks who dared pull a gun on him.

Really? This was who was attempting to rob him?

The one holding the weapon didn't even have fuzz on his damn chin, and the other one had short brown hair standing up on end.

They both stepped back.

Myles took notice of their gazes dropping down to the badge hanging around his neck.

"You'll let me live?" Myles growled. He took a step forward, using his size alone to intimidate them. He had about a good foot and almost seventy-five pounds on each of them. He was used to towering over people. With his size and build, most were afraid of him.

"Oh shit. A cop," Spikey Hair exclaimed, his eyes growing wide.

"Now, if you want this one hundred dollars, you are going to have to take it from me." Myles's lips curved up into a crooked grin—he decided to have some fun with them. He held his hand in the air, showcasing the new bills.

He dared them.

Hell, if they could get the cash from his hands, he'd give it to them freely.

"Ummm..." The gunslinger's hand shook with the weapon in it.

Doubt filled his face, and Myles almost felt bad for him. Almost.

"On second thought, I've changed my mind."

Shit, they're going to shoot someone, and it sure as hell won't be me.

"Changed your mind?" Myles scoffed. Sliding the bills into his pocket, he walked forward. "Why don't you give me this before you hurt someone." He whipped his hand out, taking the gun before the robbers could blink while brandishing his own service-issue Glock. He aimed it at them, his hand steady. "Now, I'm feeling generous right now because I don't want to be late for my meeting. I'm going to let you go and not have a few friends of mine come pick you up. Don't let me catch you on these streets again."

"Yes, sir," they both echoed in unison with their hands raised, palms facing Myles.

"Robbing a police officer at gunpoint is a serious offense, boys," Myles announced. Unlike them, he was very familiar with a gun. Most of his career in the Army had called for him be holed up in the most unforeseen areas for hours where it was nothing but him and a rifle.

Now, as a police officer and a member of the Columbia SWAT team, he was used to confrontations with guns a-blazing.

Stupid punks.

"Now go before *I* change *my* mind." Myles waved his weapon, motioning them to leave.

They took off running as if the gates of Hell had opened.

With a low chuckle, Myles slid his Glock back in its sheath.

"Idiots." He walked to his truck and got in. The gun they had pulled out on him still had the safety on. "Well, that's good." With a shake of his head, he stored it in his glove box until he could turn it in at work.

There was no telling what crimes had been committed with it.

Glancing at his watch, he released a curse.

If he didn't get a move on, he'd be late for his department meeting.

The drive to the precinct wouldn't take long.

Within fifteen minutes, Myles was striding into the station. Before going to the conference room, he'd made a pit stop and turned the confiscated gun over to

Detective Brown, who was in charge of the gun buyback program.

It was an effort that every police officer put in the time to help get guns off the streets.

"Yo, Myles!"

He turned around, recognizing the voice.

Brodie, the youngest member of their team, approached him. Brodie was the team's entry man, specializing in breaking and entering whatever building SWAT needed to go into.

"What's up, Brodie?" Myles grinned.

Brodie arrived at his side. They did the usual brotherly greeting of a fist bump and slaps on the backs.

"Shit. I think Mac makes these meetings early on purpose. Who wants to come into the office at this time of day?" Brodie shook his head, walking toward the conference room.

Myles fell in step next to him. "I know. Some of us were out late last night," Myles bragged.

"Here we go." Brodie rolled his eyes, laughing. "I need coffee so I can make sure I can process all the nasty details."

Myles barked a laugh. His night had been exciting. He'd met up with a little Spanish kitten he kept on speed dial. Nasty wouldn't even begin to describe what he'd gotten into. She'd invited over a friend, and the rest they say, is history.

He wasn't a committing man. He liked to keep his options open. Every woman he was involved with knew he wasn't the 'settling down' type. They understood he didn't offer relationships or love.

Myles, he just loved women and ensured they all enjoyed themselves in his company.

What he did bring to the table were fun-filled nights complete with passion.

He wasn't against the institution of marriage. Not at all. It was apparently working for Mac, Dec, and Ash. Had someone asked Myles if he would have thought any of his teammates would be getting married, he'd have laughed in their faces.

SWAT was a dangerous job. One that didn't come with any promises that they'd return home. Each man who wore those four letters across their chest fully understood that they would give one hundred and ten percent for their teammates.

"One day, you can be like Myles Burton," he boasted.

They arrived at the conference room, and he waved Brodie in first.

"What? Needing an STD test monthly?" Zain snickered from his corner of the room where he and Iker sat.

Chuckles went around.

Myles flipped them all off and settled into his chair next to his close friend, Ash.

This was why he loved his fellow team members. These were his brothers in blue, and being SWAT meant that he had to trust them with his life.

And he did.

Myles never thought he would have found another group of men he'd grow close with. Once he'd left the Army, he'd made sure he stayed in touch with his former unit. It wasn't like Myles had a choice. He'd spent years with them. Most times he had been deployed in the gutter of the world. Holed up in some God-forsaken part of the earth with them. He'd gone to war with those men, bled for them—killed for them.

His unit, the 25th Infantry Division of the US Army, nicknamed Hell's Devils, had been to hell and back. Their nickname was given to them while serving in Afghanistan. The unit had been deactivated, and most of the men had hung up their green berets. Some returned to civilian life while others chose the same as Myles and served in law enforcement.

Looking around the room, Myles knew there wasn't anything he wouldn't do for his current teammates.

"Don't be jealous, Zain. I'm sure we can find you a few—"

"Morning!" Mac barked, storming through the door.

Declan was right behind him.

Silence blanketed the room with the presence of their two sergeants in the place. By the expressions on Mac's and Declan's faces, there would be no joking around.

They meant business.

"Morning," the squad echoed.

Declan shut the door and took his seat in the first row. Mac walked over to the podium and laid some papers down on it. He paused and met the eyes of each man.

Mac was a tough-ass. He held the respect of every man on the team. Between him and Declan, they led their squad with an iron fist.

"SWAT tryouts are coming up tomorrow. We are potentially searching for one or two members," Mac began.

Myles sat up farther. Tryouts were an essential part of choosing a new member. They had to ensure the person would be able to not only keep up with the intense training but also fit into their close-knit group.

"What time are we to show up?" Zain asked.

"O six hundred hours," Mac replied. His gaze landed on Myles, and he gave the nod.

Myles had been charged with leading the physical endurance portion of the day.

"How many applicants?" Myles asked.

"I believe we'll have about eight who signed up," Declan answered. He turned his chair around to face the room.

Eight wasn't a bad number. Not all would survive the rigorous workout. If any of the people made it through the day, they would have the chance to progress. The second part of applying for SWAT was an interview in which they had to be invited.

Each member of the team would be responsible for assessing every applicant. The person would have to be chosen to interview with Mac and Dec. If they passed them, then the person would move up the chain of command before a decision would be made.

"Anything special you need from us, Myles?" Mac inquired.

"Just for everyone to stay sharp when observing the applicants. We're going to go through the regular drills. Let's have some fun and hopefully find our newest member." Myles glanced around the room.

It didn't need to be said that they were choosing another member of their clan. Most people didn't get to choose who was part of their family. This was the one time they could. This person would be someone who'd have to be the best at everything, someone they could trust.

SWAT's missions were perilous. A second's hesitation could cost someone their life.

This new member would need to impress the shit out of the entire team to advance.

Last year at the tryouts, no one passed on to interviews.

"Next on the agenda, I want to briefly update you on the upcoming training exercises," Mac announced.

Groans and moans went around.

Their training was a bitch. It was worth it, but there wasn't a time Myles didn't leave sore from them. To stay in top physical shape, sharp with their shooting, and ensure their endurance remained high, they had to train hard.

Myles glanced over at Ash, who grinned.

"Time for me to whoop that ass," Ash leaned over with a whisper.

Myles smiled. "Bullshit."

He and Ash were extremely competitive when it came to training courses.

"This one will be different," Mac continued.

Myles focused his attention back to his sergeant.

Different?

Mac's jaw hardened.

The tension in the air grew thick while they all waited for him to continue.

"Oh shit. Something has pissed Mac off," Brodie muttered, the only one brave enough to break the silence.

"I wouldn't say pissed off. Apparently, the governor of our beautiful state has decided to have our team assessed." Mac shoved a hand through his hair. "He's actually having all the SWAT teams in the state assessed."

Ash raised his hand. "Why? Have we done something wrong?"

"Is there a complaint against us?" Iker questioned.

Murmurs went around.

"There was an accidental shooting involving a SWAT team and a civilian who was killed." Mac paused.

The silence was deafening. As a police officer, there was no way to avoid hearing the media criticize police procedure and protocol. Most times, accidental shootings were just that—accidents.

But a few bad cops gunning down suspects had corrupted the media and turned them against the decent men and women who wore the badge proudly.

"They are bringing in a company who are the leading experts on SWAT teams. The purpose is to study us and offer expert advice to ensure we have safe weapons procedures. This is a way for us to be proactive in decreasing the chances of unwanted incidents."

Myles nodded. It sounded like a solid plan. It wouldn't hurt for them to have some outside eyes looking at them. He and the others would never be opposed to making sure they were the best at what they did.

The meeting went on with additional questioning about the assessment before Mac and Dec continued on with standard business.

"How's Deana?" Myles stood from his chair.

The meeting was adjourned, and the room began clearing out.

Ash's wide grin spoke volumes. Myles had known with one glance at Ash and Deana, that they would be perfect for each other. Myles couldn't ever remember seeing the gleam in Ash's eyes before Deana.

"She's doing great. We have about another month or so until the baby is here." Ash walked out of the conference room.

"Already?" Myles's head whipped around. "Time sure passes by fast."

They made their way through the precinct. Ash had met his fiancée at the elementary school, where he was the DARE officer. Deana was a fifth-grade teacher, and apparently, there was more to be found at the school besides kids wanting to get to know the police better.

"It does. We're almost done with the nursery. Deana got so much stuff at the baby shower. I don't know how the baby will use all of it." Ash laughed.

Myles's attention was drawn to the sight of their captain striding through the other side of the bullpen. Captain Spook was deep in conversation with a tall, older white man in a business suit. But it wasn't them who held Myles's attention.

It was the woman walking behind them.

She had long, thick hair that fell past her shoulders. She was curvy but toned, dressed in her dark business suit and heels.

Their eyes locked briefly, and Myles's tongue was stuck to the roof of his mouth. She followed the men into the captain's office.

"Who was that?" Myles cut Ash off.

They paused in place in the center of the bullpen. Now that it was later in the morning, everyone was officially at work.

"That's Earl Sutton, the owner of Logistics Intelligence Services," Ash said.

Myles turned his sights back to Ash. "How do you know?"

"His company is top-notch. I think you will also

enjoy the fact that Mr. Sutton is an Army vet, such as yourself."

Myles nodded, instantly having respect for the older man. "Who was the woman behind him?"

"Here you go." Ash shook his head with a laugh. "We are about to be audited, and you're wondering about the pretty woman?"

"Hell yeah. Did you see her?" Myles grinned. He scratched his beard. "Oh, wait. Never mind. All you can see is Deana."

"You damn right. My eyes are only for my woman," Ash agreed. He slapped Myles on the back. He swiveled and began reversing toward the front of the station. "I got to go meet Deana. She has a doctor's appointment."

"Cool. We can meet up later," Myles said.

Ash gave him a small salute before turning around.

Myles looked back at the door that led to the captain's office and sighed.

Ash was right.

They had a lot coming up, and he had to focus.

There was no time to stand around pining for a woman like he was a fifteen-year-old boy trying to draw up the courage to approach his crush.

Myles stepped from his truck and shut the door. He stalked toward the SWAT training facility. It was like a second home to him. Tomorrow, the officers attempting to join their elite group would come here.

He let himself into the large barn where they stored equipment. He didn't have much left to do to prepare.

Most of the applicants would be attempting to join for the first time. Some of the men and women wouldn't make the cut. SWAT wasn't for everyone. It took dedication, teamwork, and an understanding of what a true brotherhood meant.

There were a lot of good men on the force, but not all would be able to keep up with the training.

Myles flipped on the light and glanced around at the equipment. He remembered when he'd made the decision to try for the squad. Myles had been on the force for a year, having joined not too long after he'd returned home. There was no way he would have been able to sit around and do nothing.

He'd always planned to join a police force when he returned from serving Uncle Sam.

Myles was no dummy. He knew what it would take to be accepted on a team. He'd done it in the Army.

Once he knew when tryouts were, he began training. He'd gotten a little lax once he was out of the service.

His conditioning included running five to ten miles a day. Lifting weights and going to the range for target practice. Preparing to join the highly elite team reminded him of his days of basic training.

The need to build up his endurance again was imperative.

Myles has completed the Special Forces Sniper Course, and after years of intense training, he became a master at his craft. He was proud of his extended range technique and skills when it came to him and a high-powered rifle.

Of course, on day one, Mac had busted his balls and rode him hard. At first, Myles was lost, unsure why he was getting the wrath of the sergeant in charge. It wasn't until he learned Mac and Declan both were former SEALs and it all made sense.

They were both jealous.

That was it.

He forgave them, for not everyone was fit to be a Green Beret.

They had settled for second best and had become SEALs.

2

"Columbia SWAT is one of the most decorated squads in the state," Earl Sutton announced as they walked through the hotel front doors.

Roxxy nodded to the doorman and glanced at her father. Earl was a handsome man at the age of sixty. He was distinguished-looking with his graying hair, carefully shaved beard, and tailored suit.

"I've heard many good things about them," Roxxy replied. She widened her stride to keep up with her father's. The sound of their suitcase wheels rolling on the floor echoed through the air.

"It will do them some good to be audited and assessed. It will be our job to offer recommendations for improvement."

Roxxy nodded and followed her father to the front desk of the hotel.

Her father, a former member of the US Army, was a retired veteran who'd begun a company off of an idea he'd had. Logistics Intelligence Services was born a little over twenty years ago. He'd built their company from the ground up. Now it boasted a stellar reputation in which law enforcement agencies could trust.

Roxxy was excited to be in the city. She didn't come too often. She currently lived with her parents on the family farm that was located an hour and a half away. While here on their assignment, they would be staying in town at a hotel.

"Hello, and welcome. How may I help you?" the desk clerk asked with a smile. He was a handsome man with perfect white teeth.

"Hello, I have two rooms reserved. Last name Sutton," Roxxy announced. She leaned against the desk. Her gaze dropped down to his name badge —Ryan.

"I'll be happy to help. Let me bring up the reservation," Ryan said. His fingers flew across the keyboard. "I will need your driver's license and a credit card."

"Two rooms, huh." Her father chuckled. He pulled out his wallet and handed the requested items to Ryan. "You're too cool to share a room with your dear old dad?"

Roxxy rolled her eyes. Her father always acted like he was insulted when she didn't want to share a room with him.

"Dad..." She sighed and turned to him. She loved

her father dearly, but they worked together and lived together. She needed a little space, even if it was a hotel room while they were in town. "We go through this every single trip. You know I like to have a room to myself just to unwind and have some me time."

"We're in the city. It's not safe for a woman to stay alone," her father stressed.

Roxxy couldn't hold back her snort. She had a beautiful piece strapped to her thigh, and her suitcase held a few of her favorite guns.

She wasn't worried at all.

"Dad, I will be fine." She smiled to soften the rejection. "If it makes you feel better, you're still in the same hotel, and you taught me well."

His lips pressed firmly together while he returned her stare. "I don't like it."

"Here's your room keys" Ryan interrupted the father-daughter stare off.

Earl focused his attention to the hotel clerk to finish their check-in.

Roxxy breathed a sigh of relief.

She knew how stubborn her father was, this wouldn't be the last time she would hear this. No matter how well he'd trained her, she would always be his baby girl.

While growing up, Roxxy was the apple in her father's eye. She was the one he taught how to use a gun at the age of six. Not only had she learned to ride horses, work the farm, and get her school lessons, but she'd learned how to handle a weapon. By the age of ten, she was a sharpshooter. He'd instilled training in her as if she were one of his soldiers. By the time she was sixteen, she could easily hang with one of the many law enforcers who used their training facilities to enhance their infiltrating teams.

In reality, Roxxy didn't need protection, but in Earl Sutton's eyes, she was that young Roxxy in pigtails.

"Let's go, Roxxy." Her father turned away from the desk.

Roxxy threw a smile to Ryan and grabbed the handle of her suitcase. She pulled it behind her while she followed her father toward the bank of elevators.

They were the first to arrive in Columbia, which was the norm. She and her father usually met with the administration and squad leaders first to go over what would be expected and everything they would need to perform a full assessment. The rest of the team would arrive a day later and join them.

"Sergeant MacArthur was telling me their tryouts are tomorrow. I figured it would be good for me to attend." Roxxy stepped into the elevator.

Her father entered behind her and hit their two floors.

He ignored her statement. "Why are we on two

separate floors?" He handed her the keycard for her suite.

"Well, you always want just a standard room." She coughed. Her father was extremely frugal and never wanted to spend extra money when he deemed it not necessary. "I have a suite."

"You and your mother." He shook his head. His features softened, and he turned to her. "You are growing to be more like your mother."

"She always says I'm more like you." Roxxy gave an unladylike snort. Here she was, twenty-eight years old, and they were acting as if she were that sixteen-year-old girl.

The elevator dinged, signaling her father's floor.

"Have a good night, sweetie. Call if you need me." He leaned over and pressed a kiss to her forehead.

She melted.

She'd admit it.

She was a daddy's girl.

"Goodnight, Daddy." She smiled as he exited the car. The door closed, sealing her off from the world. She patiently focused on the numbers lighting up with each passing floor.

Roxxy couldn't help but spoil herself here and there.

She exited the elevator on the top floor and walked

down the hall. Finding her room, she entered it and shut the door behind her.

For safe measure, she flipped the latch to lock.

"Now, this is what I'm talking about." She sighed, her gaze roaming the room. It was a luxury suite with a living area decorated with the finest. She strolled through it, tossed her messenger bag on the couch, and went into the private sleeping quarters. A king bed was the star of the show. The blanket was turned down, and a little piece of chocolate was resting on the pillow. The thick comforter called to her.

Leaving her suitcase by the door, she kicked off her heels and marched over to the windows. A gasp escaped her as she took in the view of Columbia laid out before her. The city was picture-perfect. This was certainly different from the quiet country life.

"This is life." She giggled, moving away from the window. After a long day of meetings with the mayor, the captain, and the two sergeants of SWAT, she was dead on her feet. Afterward, her father had taken them out for dinner. With a full belly, she was ready to relax for the rest of the night.

She made her way into the en suite and halted in the doorway. Her mouth dropped open at the luxury in front of her. The bathroom was fit for royalty with a large clawfoot tub that could accommodate four grown adults, a stand-alone shower, and dual sinks. The marble floor sparkled.

Excited, she rushed in and began stripping her clothes off. She headed straight for the tub. She ran the water and turned to find an assortment of bath salts in a basket on the counter. With a grin, she chose the best smelling ones and tossed them in the tub.

It was officially time for her to relax.

Wrapping the plush white robe around her body, Roxxy groaned. She left the room and headed to the couch. As much as she would love to dive into the large bed and go to sleep, she did have some work to do.

Her 'break' was over.

She pulled the files out of her bag, walked back into the bedroom and settled on her bed. She switched the television on to the local news. She wanted to study the files of each member of the SWAT team, ignoring the TV. If she was to do her job thoroughly, she would need to know something about each of the men. She did take notice that there weren't any women. That wasn't part of the recommendation they could make, but it was noted.

"I'm sure there has to be a worthy woman who

could join," she muttered. She pushed down her irritation and began plowing through the paperwork.

Her gaze landed on the photograph of the man who had taken her breath away at the station.

Myles Burton.

The intensity of his eyes in the picture made her pause. She studied it, memorizing his features. He was a drop-dead gorgeous man and certainly captured her attention.

His build was something only the gods above had blessed him with. Just the memory of the way his dark t-shirt had highlighted his hard muscular chest, his dark eyes, and that bald head with a shadow of a beard on his face had her almost tripping over her feet. Roxxy was proud of her calm demeanor when she'd returned his heated gaze. Even once she'd spun away, she'd felt his eyes on her.

Just thinking of him sent her heart racing.

"Calm down, girl." She laughed, fanning herself.

Everything about him screamed the military. Roxxy didn't need to look at his file to know that.

Her eyes had immediately been drawn to him once he'd come into the bullpen with his partner. His walk was that of a predator. Being an Army brat, she was very familiar with the body language of a soldier.

Roxxy had been too busy ogling the cop that she

had missed everything her father and the captain had been speaking about.

She was just getting out of a relationship. Her ex-boyfriend, Korey Norman, had done a number on her. She had thought he had been the one, that they would spend forever together, but that wasn't the case. She'd been attracted to his deep smooth skin, his country twang, and perfect smile. There weren't many black cowboys in the area, and she was definitely drawn to the sight of him in a pair of jeans and a Stetson. The way that man sat on a horse had her heart skipping a beat.

The night she went over to his place and found another woman swallowing his cock halted all of her future dreams.

The waitress at the local diner they frequented. Roxxy had always pushed aside his harmless flirting with the woman.

"Baby, I'm just nice. I'm sure she gets a lot of assholes in here," Korey had proclaimed when she'd complained about his flirting. "You catch more flies with honey."

Roxxy had shrugged and figured he hadn't meant any harm and let him off the hook. She was with him, and the waitress was more attentive to them even when she was super busy.

One night a few weeks ago, she had thought to

surprise him. She'd just come back from an out-of-town job and let herself into his place with her key. She'd missed him and didn't want to wait until the next day to see him. It was late, but she'd figured he'd still be up.

Walking into the living room, she'd dropped her purse at the sight that greeted her.

Korey on the couch with the waitress, Anna, on her knees, sucking his dick.

Her gaze met Korey's, and he instantly pushed the woman off. He scrambled to his feet and rushed to her. Roxxy grabbed her purse and left.

For the next couple of days, Korey had tried to explain himself.

None of the excuses helped, but the one that pissed her off the most was where he put part of the blame on her and her work.

Roxxy, you're always working. There's no time for us.

His words echoed in her head.

She'd walked away from the man she'd thought she'd spend the rest of her life with, with a broken heart but her pride intact.

She would move on and find that special someone.

Someone who would love her for her.

Her gaze traveled back down to Myles Burton. His file spoke of him being a decorated member of the Special Forces. She was impressed to read he'd been a

Green Beret and had been a sniper while in the military. Continuing her reading, she learned he'd had no demerits on his record. She pulled out her notes from her conversations with Sergeant MacArthur and Owen.

Even though her father had ignored her about the tryouts, Roxxy knew that would be a perfect way to assess the team members of SWAT and their screening process.

Gathering the papers from the bed, she placed them on the nightstand. She snuggled down into the covers and pulled them over her.

She wondered if her mother remembered to give her faithful mare, Sunshine, her treats. Each night, Roxxy spoiled her horse with fresh apples. She had left a bag of freshly picked ones next to her stall. A fleeting idea came that maybe she should call her mother, but she thought twice about it.

Her mother would be insulted if Roxxy didn't trust her to take care of Sunshine.

A yawn overtook her. She rolled over onto her side and fluffed the pillow. Images of one Myles Burton filled her mind as she drifted off to sleep. Dreaming of the sexy SWAT officer wasn't a bad thing.

After what she'd been through with Korey, she'd welcome whatever naughty fantasies her brain wanted to come up with.

3

There was a crisp chill in the air while the sun hid. For Georgia, it was quite cold. Myles had covered his bald head with a black skull cap to help ward off the cold. Today was the official start of the tryouts to join their elite team. More beautiful weather would have been nice, but at least the meteorologist on the news promised it would warm up later.

Eight applicants had shown up. Not a shabby number. Their city of Columbia wasn't a vast metropolitan like Atlanta or Miami, so eight was a substantial amount.

Today, Myles and the entire squad was dressed in their full gear. The applicants were outfitted in workout clothing and lined up with Mac striding toward them.

"Good morning," Mac called out.

The seven men and one woman returned the greeting. Myles followed behind him. His gaze took in the group before him. A few of the men looked familiar, but one, in particular, stood out.

Reeves.

The young cop had tried out for SWAT before. He was an annoying little shit. He tried to fit in with the guys around the precinct, but there was something off about him. Myles didn't trust him as far as he could throw him.

Declan had shared with the group the way Reeves and his partner, Cruz, had interrogated Aspen after they had come under attack one day leaving the zoo. Reeves had threatened to handcuff Aspen instantly, earning a top spot on Declan's shit list.

"This morning, you are attempting to move forward with the process of joining our team. We will not go easy on you. When in an intense standoff, the bad guys don't give a shit about you." Mac paced back and forth, glaring at each of the men. "These men are the best, and you are vying for a spot on our team." He pointed over to the members of SWAT.

Iker, Zain, Brodie, Ashton, and Declan stood off to the side in their identical uniforms, looking every bit of the badass team they were.

"We are searching for a new member who we can trust. Someone we know who can handle the pressure when the shit hits the fan. Someone who is not afraid to charge into a hot situation." Mac paused his pacing and turned to the group. "Now this morning, Officer Myles Burton will be in charge. You are to do what he says, but know that every member of our team will be judging you."

Myles stepped in front of the line. He nodded to each of them. "Morning. We're going to start off with some physical drills to warm up. It's cold out here, and we want to get your heart pumping."

Myles's attention was drawn to the sight of a figure coming toward the group.

He swallowed hard.

It was her.

The woman from yesterday.

Myles caught Mac's eye and nodded in her direction.

Mac tipped his head and walked over to the woman.

"We're going to start off with a mile run to help get your blood flowing," Myles continued. He dragged his gaze from the woman. "Any questions?"

No one raised their hands.

"Good. Let's head over to the track." Myles pointed in the direction they needed to go.

The candidates began to head over to the field.

Myles, no longer able to contain his curiosity, went in the direction of Mac and the mystery woman who was speaking as if they'd already met each other. They turned to him once he arrived at their side.

"Speaking of him. Here he is. Myles Burton, this is Roxxy Sutton with Logistics Intelligence Services, the company who will be observing us. Roxxy, this is Myles Burton, the officer in charge of the tryouts." Mac introduced them.

"Nice to meet you, Officer Burton," Roxxy said with a southern drawl.

Myles swallowed hard, knowing he was a sucker for a country girl. He'd been raised in the north having settled in South Carolina once he'd left the Army.

"Likewise." Myles took her smaller hand in his in a firm shake. His gaze took in her smooth, light-caramel skin. Her dark hair was pulled up in a high ponytail. She didn't have on her fancy corporate suit, but today, she was dressed in cargo pants, a long-sleeved t-shirt, and dark boots. He took notice of the weapon strapped to her side and felt a stirring below the belt.

Myles was even more attracted to her.

A woman who knew her way around a gun was at the top of his wish list for his future woman.

He blinked and found he was still holding on to her hand.

"Can I have my hand back?" she asked softly with her eyebrow raised.

"Sure. I'm sorry. I don't know..." Myles released

Roxxy immediately. "Sorry. Apparently, I haven't had enough coffee today."

"Not a problem." She laughed.

Myles swallowed hard and felt Mac's curious gaze on him. He refused to turn and look at his sergeant. Myles knew without anyone telling him that this was out of character for him. He was always confident when it came to his work and women.

What the hell was his problem?

Two seconds in her presence, and he could barely remember his name.

"I take it you'll be assessing us. How can I help you?" Myles asked.

The entire team agreed they would go through the motions and pray this went by fast so they could get back to normal.

"Well, just act like I'm not here. I'm observing your screenings and protocols. We are not here to get in the way. We are truly here to help your team." Roxxy held her small clipboard close to her chest.

"Yes, we know and are open to suggestions," Mac replied. "Your company has excellent remarks and recommendations from other law enforcement agencies."

"Yes, it's something we take pride in. My father, who started the company, is an Army vet who joined the police force when he returned home," Roxxy spoke.

Myles filed that small bit of information in the back of his mind. Nothing like a good Army man with a smoking-hot daughter. Her darker complexion revealed that if her father was Caucasian then her mother must be black. Not that it mattered to Myles. He loved women no matter what their color, shape, or size. Hell, Roxxy could be purple, and he'd still be interested.

"He, too, was a SWAT officer and had the idea of a company that could help police departments and any law agencies." Roxxy broke into Myles's thoughts. "Even when he started the company, there was a lot of heat on law enforcement and their protocols. Some were unethical, and that is where our company steps in."

"Well, we are excited to have you." Mac nodded.

Myles met the gaze of his sergeant.

"I suggest you stick close to Myles. He's in charge today. The team and I will be observing and taking notes on the applicants."

Mac slapped Myles on the back and brushed past him. One look in Mac's eyes, and Myles knew Mac would want an explanation of his blunder.

"I hope you don't mind if I'm glued to your hip." Roxxy chuckled.

Her husky laugh went straight to his dick. Myles had to fight to adjust himself and pushed the carnal thoughts that were plaguing him out of his mind.

"It won't be a problem at all, ma'am." His gaze dropped down and slowly made its way along her curvy body until he reached her combat boots. They were small and dark and would be deemed cute. His eyes flickered back to hers.

He didn't care that she'd caught him.

He was never one to bite his tongue when he saw a woman he was interested in.

Hell, he was more than interested.

He wanted to pick her up and toss her over his shoulder and leave.

Fuck the tryouts.

Her eyes darkened, and it was as if she had the same thoughts. Myles hadn't missed when she'd taken advantage of Mac speaking and quickly checked him out.

"Shall we?" She cocked her perfectly sculpted eyebrow up high.

"Yes." He coughed. He had forgotten about the new recruits waiting for him. "Please follow me." He turned on his heel and scrubbed at his face. "I'm sure you've read up on how applicants apply?"

"Yes, I familiarized myself with all of the current

members of your team, the policies and protocols of applying for SWAT here."

She'd read his file?

Myles instantly wanted to know what she'd thought.

It had been a while since he'd reviewed what was on him.

"I'd have to say I'm impressed with you, Officer Burton." She fell in step with him.

He slowed down, slightly sensing her shorter legs.

"Really?" A grin spread on his lips.

Of course she would have read his file.

What was he worried about?

"Yes. I'm a little partial to men who were in the Army." She laughed.

"Is that so?"

"Yes, I was an Army brat, so you could say the Army is in my blood."

They arrived where everyone else was waiting on them. Myles wished they had more time to talk alone. He made a promise to himself that by the time the day was over, he'd be asking her out, and if he played his cards right, by nightfall, they'd be alone but would be having a different kind of conversation.

"All right, men," Myles barked out. He instantly grew serious and glared at the recruits. "I hope you've gone ahead and stretched out good."

"Yes, sir," the group echoed.

"Let's line up," he instructed.

He walked to the edge of the track while they took their places behind the starting line. His teammates were in the center of the field so they could keep an eye on the applicants. He trusted that each of them would be making mental notes on the men and the woman attempting to join their team. At the end of the day, they would meet to discuss what they'd seen. If any of the men or the female captured the team's interest, then they would be invited for phase two, the interviews. "On your mark. Get set. Go!"

The men and lady took off jogging. They would need to set a steady pace. His team called out encouragement and clapped for the recruits. Even though they weren't already on the team, SWAT was a brotherhood. They instantly supported anyone trying to join them.

Once the recruits finished their laps, Myles led them to their next activity.

Push-ups.

"All right, recruits. You will be timed. One hundred push-ups is all we ask. This should be easy for you since you don't have all your gear on," Myles taunted them.

"Let's see you drop and give us fifty, Burton," a familiar voice called out.

Myles turned to find Ash grinning at him.

"I mean, we are making them do it without gear on. Let's show them what we're looking for."

"Fifty?" Myles scoffed. He felt Roxxy's eyes on him. His typical cocky attitude was breaking through. He always loved attention. He hadn't worked hard on his body for nothing. "Fuck. I can do a hundred," he bragged.

The men all chuckled around him.

"Let's show these recruits what a real SWAT member can do." Ash came to stand next to him.

Everyone formed a circle around Myles who loved the attention.

"Get on the ground, Soldier."

Myles jumped around on the balls of his feet. He whipped his arms back and forth, knowing that doing push-ups with about eighty pounds of equipment was much different than with only his weight. The pressure was on, but it wasn't anything he couldn't handle.

Hell, this was nothing compared to when he was in the Army.

Getting down in position, Myles waited for Ashton.

"And go!" Ash glanced at his watch.

Myles instantly dropped down and pushed himself up. He started rapidly completing the push-ups until he found a good steady rhythm. Sweat formed and ran down his face, but he kept going.

Myles Burton wasn't a punk.

He would do one hundred push-ups in front of his team.

Challenging each other wasn't new. That was a common thing with the guys. It was the camaraderie amongst them that kept them close. The current members of SWAT cheered him on.

"Eighty, eighty-one, eighty-two," they counted aloud for him.

He released a curse, feeling himself slow down.

His muscles burned and shook, but he refused to give up. His movements fell in sync with their counting.

"Ninety, ninety-one, ninety-two," they continued.

"Finish strong, Burton," Mac growled near him. His sergeant knelt on the ground next to him. "Push through the pain," he ordered.

Myles growled and pulled strength from deep within him and kept going.

"Ninety-eight, ninety-nine...one hundred!"

Myles shoved off the ground and flexed his arms. "Woo!" he shouted, whipping his cap off. Before it had helped keep the chill from him, and while he'd been doing push-ups, it kept the sweat from sliding into his eyes, but now, he was hot.

The applause went around. Myles's team members slapped him on the back. Myles laughed as the guys taunted him. His eyes connected with Roxxy's, and he threw her a wink before turning back to the recruits.

"All right, people. Let's get to it."

4

Roxxy had to force herself to concentrate. She couldn't stop thinking of Myles and those damn push-ups. Something so simple as watching him working out had her body going haywire. His cockiness shined through.

That grin of his.

The wink.

Calm down, girl.

She followed the group over to the shooting range. The recruits were instructed to put on gear for the shooting exercise. They had completed their push-ups, sit-ups, and pull-ups. With each test, one of the SWAT guys was challenged and had to do the task with their full gear on. Roxxy had to give it to the members of Columbia SWAT, they were a close group. She could see it in the way they taunted yet supported each other. They cracked jokes on one another while ribbing each other.

The recruits walked over to a barn that was next to the outdoor range.

"Officer Burton." She stepped over to him and had to beg her body to behave. Standing close to him meant her nipples instantly hardened. She collapsed her clipboard to her chest and stopped next to him. "I have a question."

"Yes, Mrs. Sutton?"

His dark gaze bored into her, taking her breath away. A small smile broke out on her lips.

"It's not Mrs. That would be my mother," she corrected him with a shake of her head. "It's Miss."

"Hmm..."

His gaze narrowed on her, and her core clenched. Roxxy bit back a curse. She'd just fallen for one of the oldest tricks in the book. He was testing out if she was married. His gaze swept her body again, and she practically melted. Why was her body so strung? Myles Burton was dangerous. Cocky. Good-looking. Muscular and fit. *Shit.* She was a sucker for a man with muscles.

"How can I help you, Miss Sutton?"

Don't answer truthfully. Don't you dare, Roxxy Lynn Sutton, answer him.

"What is the purpose of the recruits donning vests and other equipment for the shooting exercises?" she answered. She breathed a sigh of relief that her lips didn't betray her.

"It's much easier to shoot a gun with regular clothes on and having time to aim and shoot. We train the way we go out on real calls. We have to increase the pressure to make sure everyone is capable of handling their own under intense situations. You don't get a chance to think while out in the field."

Roxxy nodded in complete understanding. "It's good to train as if you are out in the field."

She scribbled a few notes down. Glancing up, she stared at the targets then turned back to Myles. "I want to shoot."

"Excuse me?" His eyebrows rose high.

"Put me through the shooting test." She capped her pen. There was no better way to learn about the team than to jump right in the middle. It had been a few days since she'd shot a gun. "I want to get a feel of the weapons you have them use, the targets, the distance, and how you put them under pressure."

"I thought you were just here to observe?" Myles rested his hands on his hips.

His skeptical look fueled her desire to bust his balls a little. This man, gorgeous specimen that he was, needed to be taken down a peg or two.

She was the right one for the job.

Sergeants MacArthur and Owen arrived at their side.

"What's wrong?" MacArthur asked, obviously sensing the tension between them.

"She wants to be put through the shooting drill." Myles smoothed a hand over his bald head.

MacArthur and Owen turned their gazes to her before focusing on Myles.

"No harm. Miss Sutton's here to get a feel of our screening process, then suit her up," Sergeant Owen said.

"I agree. She's here to study our process and protocols, let Roxxy shoot." Mac shrugged.

"Thank you, Sergeants MacArthur and Owen." She nodded to both of them.

"If you are going to be here for a while, you might as well call me Mac," Mac replied gruffly.

"And I'm just Dec or Declan." Declan chuckled. "Calling us sergeants is too formal."

Roxxy faced Myles, who was still studying her. A tremor slid down her back from his intense gaze that had nothing to do with the slight chill in the air.

"You can handle a gun, right?" Myles's gaze dropped down to her firearm.

His lips curved up into a smirk that almost had her stepping forward and whacking him on the arm. Instead, she glared at him and had to bite her lip to keep from saying anything unprofessional and certainly unladylike.

"Watch me, Officer Burton. The barn is where I can grab what I need, right?" she asked, haughtily pointing at the building.

Once he nodded, she turned on her heel and stormed away.

Myles Burton didn't know who he'd just pissed off.

Could she handle a gun?

Roxxy released a snort and marched her way toward the barn.

"She's pissed at you." Dec chuckled, slapping Myles on the back.

"What did I say?" Myles turned around, completely clueless. He'd asked an appropriate question. Just because she had a weapon on her didn't mean anything. He never wanted to assume someone was capable of handling a firearm. There were plenty of women and men who walked around with guns but didn't know how to safely use them.

"If looks could kill, you'd be pushing up daisies." Mac shook his head.

"Was I wrong for asking her?" Myles folded his arms against his chest.

"She's with the company which is to audit us and advise where we are lacking. I'm betting she can shoot the pants off any of the recruits." Declan waved to the men exiting the barn.

"Hell, I'd be willing to bet she'd a better shot than Myles." Mac grinned.

"Now that's something I'll wager—"

"Hey." Myles held his hand up. What the fuck? Shoot better than him? Did they all forget who he was? He had been a fucking sniper in the Army. During missions for SWAT, if they needed a target taken out from a distance, it was him who was the go-to person for it. "First of all, she may be able to shoot better than the recruits, but I'm sure as hell putting my money on her shooting better than you two Navy boys."

Dec and Mac turned to Myles. Their smiles disappeared. Yup, this Army soldier would be down to bet against his sergeants.

"What's going on over here?" Brodie jogged over and joined them.

Myles turned to his fellow teammate, who was also a proud Army man. Brodie had served and did two tours before his discharge. He was the youngest member of their team, having joined a few years ago. Myles had immediately taken him under his wing once he'd learned Brodie had served in the Army.

Army men stuck together.

"I think your teammate here was about to put his foot in his mouth," Mac warned. The corners of his mouth edged up, and his eyes narrowed on Myles.

Both he and Declan adjusted their stance, facing Myles and Brodie.

"Not at all. See here, Brodie." Myles put his arm around Brodie's shoulder and laughed. "These two Navy men think that just because they are our superiors, we wouldn't want to wage a little bet."

"Is that so." Brodie rubbed his hands together. "What are we betting on?"

Myles grinned. "You know the woman who is observing us?"

"How could I not?" Brodie gave a long, low whistle. "She's a fox. All the guys have been talking about her since she arrived."

Myles bit back a growl. *All the guys?*

"Well anyway," he continued, shaking his head. Why would he care that the other men on the grounds found her attractive? Sure, she had a flawless, smooth light complexion, thick dark hair that he wanted to see flowing over her naked shoulders...

Myles blinked.

Naked shoulders.

Where the hell did that come from?

He had to push the fantasy of a naked Roxxy out of his mind quick.

"Anyway," he repeated. "They are willing to wager how well Miss Sutton shoots. They say better than me, which we all know would be damn near impossible," he scoffed.

Brodie barked a hard laugh with him. Mac and Declan glared at him, both folding their arms in front of their chests.

"I say she shoots better than them."

"For us to settle this, it would mean all three of you would have to participate and shoot along with the recruits," Brodie said.

The men of SWAT were downright competitive when it came to anything.

Today was no different.

Looked like Myles was about to enter a shooting contest with his sergeants.

"Let's do it." Declan said. "Myles is a sniper. Someone who has to plan and strategize to hit a target meters away. This is active shooting at the drop of a hat. You don't have time to think."

"Aim, pull the trigger, and hit the bull's-eye," Mac finished. He raised an eyebrow. "Think you can do that better than us? Bring it."

"And the wager?" Brodie stepped back a foot, his gaze flickering back and forth between Myles, Declan, and Mac. He was officially the referee.

"If I shoot a better score than these two right

here..." Myles tried to think of something. Their wagers were always somewhat senseless. They never gambled for money when competing. "My truck could use a good wash and detailing."

Declan rolled his eyes. "Didn't you just go off-roading?"

"Maybe." Myles grinned. His truck had more mud on it that one would have trouble seeing what color it was.

"That's fine." Declan chuckled. "Mac, weren't you just saying you needed to stain your deck?"

Myles groaned, running a hand along his head. Mac's deck on the back of his house was pretty significant. It was able to accommodate the entire team once a quarter when they had their infamous cookouts at his home. "Okay, okay. That's doable."

"And if she shoots better than Myles..." Mac gave a dramatic pause. He scrubbed a palm over his jawline, his eyes shifting to the barn. He turned back and met Myles's head-on. "If she does better than Myles, then he has to ask her out on a date."

Myles's mouth dropped open in shock.

"I have to do what?" he sputtered. Ask Roxxy out? Was Mac crazy?

Declan and Brodie fell out in a fit of laughter. Mac's gaze was unwavering.

"You heard me," Mac said. "She beats you, then

you have to ask her out on a date. What's the harm in that? With how you just insulted her, I'm sure the answer would be no anyway."

"Come on, Mac, think of something else." Miles groaned. There was no way he would be asking her out. As much as he secretly wanted to, he was sure there were some rules against one of the cops she was observing taking her out.

"What? Is Myles Burton afraid of a woman?" Mac goaded him.

Myles instantly stood to his full height. "Myles Burton isn't afraid of anything."

"Then what's so hard about asking her out?" Mac shrugged.

"He got you there, Myles." Brodie chuckled. He wiped the trail of laughter tears from his face.

Myles glared at him. They were supposed to be on the same side.

"I think Myles may have finally met his match." Declan snickered. "When has Myles ever not wanted to go out with a beautiful woman?"

"Okay, okay." Myles raised both hands in defeat. He would ask the woman out. Once Roxxy said no, then he would have held up his part of the wager.

But first, he wasn't planning on losing.

He needed his truck cleaned and detailed.

"You motherfuckers got yourselves a deal."

5

Roxxy was fitted with the same gear as the recruits. A ballistic vest, protective eyewear, and a standard-issue Glock. Marching toward the group, she caught sight of Myles speaking with his fellow teammates, Ashton and Brodie. She tried to keep the scowl from forming, but it was a losing battle.

Did she know how to handle a weapon?

She arrived at the range where the men stood waiting for their instructions. The sky was clear, and the air still crisp. It was beautiful outside, and they couldn't have picked a better day.

The recruits were lined up in front of their own aisle, where they would step up to the marker. Roxxy marched over to the empty row. Lucky number seven.

"Okay, here we are going to test your endurance with the shooting. We are going to put a little pressure on you. In real life, the bad guys will shoot you and not think twice about it." Myles walked in front of them, pausing a few feet from her. His eyes darkened, and a smirk appeared on his lips. "We are not going to take it easy on you. We will try to distract you, yell at you, be all over you."

Roxxy swallowed hard with the fantasy that appeared before her.

All over her?

Fuck.

What she wouldn't give to have Myles Burton all over her.

She shook her head, trying to clear her thoughts. Myles turned around and walked back the way he'd come while he continued speaking.

"On my command, you will pull your weapon and fire at the target. We are looking for precision. Someone who can remain in control and hit the targets, because you know what?" He paused and glanced at each one of them. "The bad guys certainly won't miss."

"We are going to give a demonstration as always." Mac stepped forward.

Roxxy took notice that other members of the team had come along. He, Declan, and Myles each moved up to the line in front of three of the targets.

Roxxy witnessed how the recruits were paying attention. They were focused, and a few of them, she could tell they really wanted to join the elite group. Conversations in the barn hinted at that. They all had much respect for the team that they were vying for a spot on.

"Pay attention, ladies and gentlemen," Declan announced.

The tension in the air thickened. Roxxy was left in the dark, not knowing if they were indeed about to demonstrate because they wanted to, or if they had a little competition going on. She would think that one demonstration would be enough. Shrugging, she decided to ask later, but for now, she'd watch the show.

Two of the team surrounded Mac, who went first. His jaw hardened, and his eyes narrowed on the target. His fierce gaze had her glad she would never be on the receiving end of such a stare. The men goaded him, yelled at him while he pulled his gun from its holster and fired a full round at the target.

This time Declan went. Same deal. Two men stood on each side of him, antagonizing him, yelling, trying to break his laser focus. He, too, emptied an entire round without so much as a flinch.

"All right, Burton. Your turn," Ashton called out.

He and the one named Iker surrounded Myles, who rolled his shoulders before bracing himself.

Roxxy was unsure why, but her breath caught in her throat. He whipped out his weapon and fired. He, like Mac and Declan, had a fierce focus. No matter how loud and obnoxious Iker and Ashton were, his gaze didn't waver from the target.

The recruits clapped at the end of the demonstration. Roxxy joined them, impressed with the show of marksmanship.

"Anyone can shoot a gun," Myles began. He turned while securing his weapon back at his side. His gaze roamed the recruits and landed on Roxxy. "As was stated before, we are looking for precision while under pressure."

"Not bad, men," Brodie announced, walking over to the targets.

"Who shot better?" a deep voice called out.

Chuckles went around. Roxxy tried to hold back the roll of her eyes. Of course, the men would be competing.

She should have known.

It didn't matter that these were strong men who faced danger daily.

Put a gun in their hands, and a target a few feet away, and those men morphed into hormonally driven teens.

"Looks like the winner is..." Brodie walked back and forth between the three targets. "Myles."

Myles grinned as he rotated. He brandished his biceps and flexed them, showing off.

Jesus, the man was cocky and built.

Even through his dark clothing, the well-defined muscles stood out. Each of the SWAT men were chiseled and built, but it was Myles who certainly captured her attention.

Her heart skipped a beat.

She would love to be the one running her hands over the contoured lines of every ridge of his hardened body.

"Okay, now, recruits, your turn. Smith, you're up first," Myles called out, breaking through her carnal fantasies.

Roxxy waited, watching as each recruit was put through the strain of shooting. A few held themselves together, while others weren't ready at all for shooting under pressure. They made her last since she wasn't officially trying out, and she was okay with that. While they tested each person, she mentally took notes.

"Okay, Miss Sutton. You're next," Myles's deep voice sounded beside her.

She met his gaze with a stubborn one of her own. She wasn't going to let him intimidate her at all. His devilish good looks, muscles, and the fact she had to tilt her head back just to meet his gaze—she'd shove all of that to the side.

Focus, Roxxy.

He wasn't going to distract her at all.

"Let's do it, Officer." She thickened her drawl on

purpose and stepped forward to the mark where she was to stand.

She bit back a smile, sensing his gaze on her back. She pushed her protective glasses up on the bridge of her nose. He arrived at her left while Brodie stood to her right. Focusing on the target, she rested her hand around the cold steel of the issued Glock. "Ready when you are, sir."

Myles stiffened next to her.

Roxxy knew she had him.

Her heart rate decreased while she concentrated on the bull's-eye. Being the only one of two females amongst all these men was enough stress as it was.

She blew out a deep breath.

It wasn't as if the fate of all womanhood rested on her shoulders.

She just had to shoot a gun and hit the targets.

And not think of Mr. Tall, Dark, and Handsome next to her.

"Shoot the target, Sutton," Myles ordered.

Willing her heart to slow, she gripped the Glock and drew it from the sheath. She brought it up in front of her and held it steady in her two hands. She aimed and pulled the trigger. She was ready for the recoil of the weapon after it fired.

"Where's she learn to shoot a gun, cheerleading practice?" Brodie snapped.

He and Myles continued to berate her, trying to throw off her concentration.

She filed that first comment in the back of her mind for later. The two men tried to get under her skin.

But she was Earl Sutton's daughter.

Her hand remained steady while she continued firing the weapon.

"No cheerleader I've ever known would be caught dead with a gun in their hands." Myles laughed.

"With your reputation, I'm sure you know a lot of cheerleaders." Brodie snorted. "Remember that time you were telling us the story of—"

"Done." Roxxy cut Brodie off. She stood straight and secured her borrowed weapon.

He had a reputation with women.

Of course he does. Roxxy held back an unladylike grunt.

"Good job, Sutton," Myles remarked. He gave her a short nod and stepped back away from her.

"Thanks," she murmured. Her skin tingled from the eyes of the men surrounding her.

"Nice shooting, Miss Sutton." Brodie jogged over to the targets.

Roxxy patiently waited for Brodie to announce what she already knew.

"Holy fuck!" Brodie exclaimed as he examined her target sheet.

"Well." Mac strolled toward them. "We're all wanting to know."

Roxxy glanced at Mac, unsure why they would all want to know what she'd shot. Her gaze landed on Myles, who was not hiding the fact he was staring at her. Turning her attention back to Brodie, she waited again.

"She hit the bull's-eye on every shot but one," Brodie called out.

She shrugged with a glance at Myles.

No one was perfect.

She hadn't liked the fact that he knew lots of cheerleaders. That little bit of knowledge threw her off. She was unsure why, but she was ready to gouge out the eyes of every single cheerleader he knew.

The applause went up in the air. Roxxy gazed around with pride filling her chest. She smiled and nodded to the men as they gazed upon her with admiration and respect.

The one female cop gave her the thumbs-up. Her smile widened, having shared a brief moment with her fellow woman.

"Seems like she does know how to handle a gun." Declan laughed. He slapped Myles on the back and shook his head. "Hell, you looking for a job?"

Roxxy smirked at the sight of Myles rolling his eyes.

"Not at the moment, but if I ever get bored with what I'm currently doing, I'll keep you guys in mind."

"Let's give it up for Myles leading today's tryouts." Mac clapped.

The team joined in. Myles nodded to each of his men.

"We had a good group this year. I thank each of you for coming out to participate," Myles said. Even though it was required for each team member to join in the observation process, he knew his men would have been there anyway. Choosing a new member of SWAT was a group decision. Every man had to be sure about the new member.

This decision was to be made together.

"I want you to think long and hard. Anyone you think should deserve a shot at an interview?" Mac asked the group.

They stood in a circle away from the barn as the recruits returned their gear.

Myles's mind was filled with Roxxy and her determined glare. The way she held the gun in her hands and her almost perfect aim. He almost wished she needed help with aiming. He would have loved nothing more than to stand behind her and wrap his arms around her to show her how to hold a gun properly.

"Burton!" a voice snapped.

Myles blinked and turned to Declan. "What?"

"Did you even hear what we said?" Declan cocked an eyebrow high.

"He's probably trying to figure out how to ask Roxxy out." Ash grunted.

Chuckles went around. Myles rolled his eyes and stood straighter. He could take their teasing. He was a big boy.

"Honestly, I was thinking of Gizzy," he murmured. He swept a hand over his jaw.

Ash narrowed his eyes on Myles. Gizzy was Ash's single sister, who was a teacher at a nearby school district.

"Excuse me. What did you say?" Ash took a step toward him.

Myles couldn't help but bust his friend's balls. "You found love at an elementary school. I think I may take a crack at it. What grade does Gizzy teach again?"

Myles barked a laugh when Ash dove at him. Zain and Iker caught him by the arms. He wasn't afraid of his friend. It wouldn't be the first time one of the men on the team got into a squabble.

"That's enough, men," Mac barked, irritation lining his face.

"He's just messing with you," Iker laughed. He pushed Ash back into Zain. Iker glanced over at Myles. "Tell him you're pulling his chain."

"Ash, man, you know I love Gizzy like a sister." Myles chuckled and shook his head. She was as cold as her brother. There were no sparks between Gizzy and Myles. He considered her one of the fellas. "None of us would dare to go near your sister."

"We're good?" Declan asked Ash.

"Yeah. We're good." Ash shook Zain off him and straightened his clothes. He sent a frosty glare to Myles before turning his attention back to their two sergeants.

Myles rolled his eyes, knowing he'd have to personally apologize to his friend.

"Back to what I was saying. We need to decide if anyone deserves to move forward with the interview process." Mac folded his arms in front of his chest. "Zain. What do you think?"

"I think Knight has potential. I liked her form. She transferred in from Atlanta from what I know," Zain responded.

Myles thought of the new woman and mentally agreed with Zain. Jordan Knight was new to their precinct, having transferred sometime last year. Myles didn't know much about the patrol officer but had been impressed by what he'd seen out on the field.

"I second Zain." Iker raised his hand. "I've heard nothing but good things about Knight. She's solid. When I knew she was trying out, I put in a couple calls with a few friends over at her old precinct. Everyone had great things to say about her."

"Myles. What say you?" Mac directed his attention to Myles.

"I liked what I saw today. Knight seems like a solid gal. Cracked a few jokes. I say, let her move on to the interview process."

Once a cop was able to advance to interviews, they turned the heat on. Everything in their file would be combed over. The person would even be allowed to train with the SWAT team which would allow them all to really feel out the recruit.

They continued around the group, with each man speaking about the potentials. It seemed like everyone felt something good about Officer Knight.

"All right then. Looks like we have our answer." Declan clapped his hands together. Murmurs of agreement went around. "Now, our Myles lost a bet."

Myles groaned, scuffing a hand across his cheek. "I didn't actually lose the bet."

"If I recall, there was a stipulation that if she shot better than you..." Brady shrugged.

Myles glared at him. They were supposed to be on the same side.

"I'm sorry," Brady mouthed back to him.

Of course, they would want him to approach her now.

Mac gave a low chuckle and pushed his sunglasses on top of his head. "I mean, if you are too chicken to complete the mission, Burton, I'm sure some of our other single team members won't hesitate to—"

"I'm going to do it," Myles ground out. The thought of another man approaching Roxxy had him wanting to slam his fist into any of his teammate's faces.

He paused.

Where the hell this aggression come from? He glanced around and found each of their eyes on him. Zain, Iker, Ash, Dec, Brody, and Mac, all staring at him in shock.

"Look who's walking out the barn now." Ash nodded toward the building.

Roxxy sauntered out, speaking to Reeves and Brown. Myles narrowed his eyes on the way she held her clipboard to her chest. The smile that graced her lips was being wasted on the two men beside her. They were practically salivating on her as they held on to whatever she was saying.

"Well, while you decide on how you're going to do it, lover boy, I need to speak to her about her findings for the day." Mac gave the group a salute before heading over to her.

Myles had never had issues asking a woman out. Especially not in front of his friends. He'd left many bars with a woman or two when they had all gone out drinking.

Why was he hesitating now?

What was so different about Roxxy?

6

"Who taught you to shoot like that?" Officer Reeves asked.

His grin widened, and Roxxy had to hold back from rolling her eyes.

She smiled and shook her head. She was used to men always being in awe that a woman could outshoot them. It was the stereotypical question, and Reeves was no different than most men she came into contact with when she was working the major city precincts.

"My daddy taught me to shoot when I was a youngin," she drawled, letting her southern roots show. Out in the country, girls grew up practically with a shotgun in hand. City boys never really understood that.

"Wow. Looks like I need to take my ass down to the range more often." Officer Brown laughed.

He appeared to be a shy man who Roxxy learned had been on the force about ten years and was ready to advance to something more than a patrolman.

"I used to live in our local ones. But then we live on a farm, so I have my own personal shooting range. Dad and I used to be out there for hours on days," Roxxy shared.

Those were the great memories.

She and her father shot any and everything he put up as targets.

Her mother scolded both of them when chores got behind.

"If you don't make SWAT, then what would you do?" she asked. It was a valid question that she needed to know for their evaluation. Most people didn't make SWAT, and one thing they liked to report to the leadership was the aspirations of their employees.

"Well, if I don't make it, it won't be a bad thing. This is my first time trying out, and it definitely taught me that I am not in shape like I thought I was." Brown laughed again.

Roxxy chuckled with him. At least he was realistic.

"Hell, if I don't make it, I have my eye on a few other units. I just want to find my place."

Roxxy nodded, having respect for him. It was good he realized that not everyone fit in certain groups. He was lucky he was on one of the police forces that had a lot to offer their policemen and women.

"Me, I'm sure I'll make SWAT." Reeves preened.

Roxxy glanced at him in surprise. For some strange

reason, he was confidently sure of himself. When she'd observed him, he wasn't the best candidate. The physical part he'd nailed, but when it came to shooting, he was off.

"I tried out last year and didn't make it."

"And you're sure because of that, they'll pick you?" she asked. She failed to hide her astonishment.

Reeves folded his arms across his chest with a cocky grin on his lips. "I'm sure of it. I've trained hard since last year. I've memorized all there is to learn and know about being on the team. I know all of the guys, and I'm sure they're cool with me." He shrugged as if he didn't have a care in the world.

"They choose the best person for the fit for the team." Brown rolled his eyes.

"And that's me." Reeves laughed.

Roxxy shook her head at the two. She turned and saw Mac making his way to her. Right behind him was Myles. Her heart instantly stuttered when her gaze was met by Myles's dark eyes.

"Miss Sutton," Mac greeted her.

Reeves and Brown both quieted down as the sergeant stopped next to them. They both were horrible at masking their emotions on their faces. Hope and admiration.

Roxxy seriously doubted either of them would make the team. There were maybe two potentials she could see, advancing to the next step, but these two officers weren't her choices.

"Sergeant," she murmured with a nod. She plainly ignored Myles and didn't offer a greeting to him.

She caught his grin out the corner of her eyes, and she had to bite her tongue from snapping at him.

Could she handle a gun?

Ha! I showed him!

"If you don't mind, men, we'd like to talk to Miss Sutton alone for a few minutes. You two can go over with the others. Sergeant Owen will be updating the group in a few minutes." Mac didn't even look their way when dismissing them. He was one hard-ass SWAT leader, and the results of his leadership showed.

The team was a stellar one, and their bond was unlike anything she'd ever seen before.

"Yes, sir," Reeves and Brown echoed. They headed in the direction where the other recruits were waiting.

"How soon will your reports be ready?" Mac asked.

"The way our reporting works is that once we have completed our full assessment, your captain will receive the initial reports. It will be up to him when he gives you a copy," she replied.

Mac's narrowed gaze on her spoke volumes.

"What's an average amount of time we should

expect once the assessment has been completed?" Myles asked.

She gripped her clipboard tighter and turned a frosty glare to him. "Whenever I'm done with it. We at Logistics Intelligence pride ourselves on our thoroughness. We still have a lot to go through around here. But as soon as we have completed our assessment, the reports will be on the captain's desk."

"We mean no disrespect, Miss Sutton." Mac held up his hands, apparently trying to defuse the situation. He glanced at both of them wearily. "We are just looking for a timeframe. This is serious for us. We'd like to know where there are areas of improvement. What your company recommends could save a life."

Roxxy blew out a deep breath. He was right to want to know when to expect reports. This was their first evaluation. She shouldn't take out her anger toward Myles on him or the team.

But Myles Burton rubbed her the wrong way.

Or maybe she wanted him to rub her the right way.

His dark eyes were locked on her. Deep in them, she could see he got a kick from getting a rise out of her.

Cocky son of a bitch.

He was doing this on purpose.

Why did he have to be so gorgeous?

Why couldn't he be butt ugly or act like an ass to her?

Instead, he asked a straightforward question, and it set her off.

"Normally, once we complete an assessment, we have the reports to the captain in about two weeks." This time she answered calmly. Her voice was neutral and didn't shake. She was proud she was able to damper her anger so quickly. She could be a hothead, and now was not the time to show that side of her off. "But please know that if we do pick up on something that would put a person in danger, we notify the captain and the squad leaders immediately so that corrective action could be started as soon as possible."

Mac nodded, seeming satisfied with her answer. "Well, that's more what I was looking for. I think it's good that your company is here going through our protocols and procedures."

Myles remained silent, and the hairs on her arms rose. The temperature outside had warmed up, and there wasn't that slight chill anymore. Even with the sun beaming down on them, she had goosebumps on her arms from his stare. She was thankful for her clipboard. Keeping it close to her body allowed her to hide how she was reacting to him. Her nipples were hard and pushing against her bra. The material was irritating them, and she would kill to be able to strip her clothes off.

With Myles.

Alone in her hotel room.

What the hell?

Get a grip, girl, she snapped to herself.

"Are you done here today?" Mac asked.

"Actually, I am. I think I'm about to head over to the precinct to meet with my colleagues."

"Let us know if you need anything else. Any of the men would be willing to answer any questions," Mac volunteered.

"Actually, that would be perfect. I do want to meet with each of you sometime this week."

"You let us know, and I'll make sure we're there." Mac stepped forward and offered her his hand.

She took it in a firm shake.

He stepped back and turned to Myles, slapping him on the shoulder. "See that she gets to her car safe, Burton."

Roxxy's mouth dropped open, and she watched the sergeant walk away. She could see herself to her car. It wasn't that far away and parked in the small lot where all of their vehicles were. She doubted anything would happen to her on police-owned grounds.

"Yes, sir," Myles with a wide grin spreading.

"I assure you that I'm just fine walking to my car."

She huffed, turned on her heel, and headed toward the parking lot.

"I have orders. You heard them," Myles gloated.

She could hear the smile in his words. She clenched her teeth and keep going. He caught up to her and fell in line with her. She noticed how he had to shorten his strides to match hers.

"I'm sure a man like yourself has disobeyed an order or two before." She sniffed.

"Never."

Her gaze flew to his to find him serious. No smile. No joking.

"A soldier always follows the commands of his superiors."

"But you're not in the Army any longer, Officer Burton."

They made their way around to the front building on the training grounds and to the parking lot.

"Doesn't matter."

Myles's deep voice sent a chill down her spine. She had to force herself to remember that she was pissed at him.

"My sergeant gave me an order, I'll follow through."

Damn military men and their honor and orders. She grew up with an Army man for a father, and Earl Sutton was as stubborn as they come.

She should have known Myles would be no different.

It must be something they drilled into them once they entered the service.

"Well, thank you for escorting me to my car," she said haughtily. She walked around her dark sedan and stopped at the driver's door. Using her keypad, she entered her code to unlock it. She opened the door and tossed her clipboard onto the passenger seat.

"You're quite welcome." Myles strolled around the vehicle toward her.

Roxxy straightened to find Myles standing behind her. She tilted her head back to meet his gaze. "Is there something else you need from me?"

She cringed on the inside, hearing the huskiness in her voice.

His eyes darkened, and she watched as he licked his lips.

Her core clenched at the sight of his tongue sneaking out.

"Look, Roxxy. I know I pissed you off, but I truly didn't mean to."

He had a serious look on his face, and she felt the walls she thought she had constructed, crumble.

"I would have asked the same question to anyone. It's about safety around here. Pure and simple."

"I...uh, I understand." She let out a sigh and

pushed a few wayward strands of hair behind her ear. "I guess I can admit I overreacted a little."

His eyebrows rose high. "A little?"

She laughed, covering her face with her hands, her cheeks warm with humiliation. "Okay, maybe a lot."

"How about this." His fingers gently pried hers from her face. He stepped closer to her, just a hair's breadth away from her. Her hands fell apart, but Myles's larger ones still held on to hers. "Let me make it up to you. Tonight, have dinner with me."

Her breath caught in her throat. She swallowed hard.

Should she?

Her mind raced, and she could think of about eight reasons why she shouldn't go out with him.

"Myles, I don't think—"

"You just said that you wanted time to speak with each SWAT member, right?" he asked. He was smooth. Real smooth.

She bit her lip and stared at him.

He nonchalantly shrugged. "You want to interview me, and you have to eat."

Dammit, he was stroking her hand with his thumb, and it sent a rush of arousal through her body. It had been a minute since a member of the opposite sex not related to her had touched her.

"Myles—"

"You don't eat?" he cut her off, not giving her a chance to complete her sentence. He closed the gap between them, and her breasts were pushed against the hard plane of his chest.

The scent of his cologne was like an aphrodisiac. She breathed in deeply, mesmerized by the smell of him.

"Of course I do," she spluttered. The heat of Myles's body radiated through his dark shirt. He'd taken off his gear after the final leg of the tryouts, leaving her to feel him.

Myles was one hundred percent all man.

She bit back a moan at the feel of his hardened chest.

Rigid abdomen...and if she didn't know any better, she would swear he had a long flashlight hidden in his jeans pressing close to her.

"Well, then it's a deal."

"Um, okay," she breathed. She watched with bated breath as Myles leaned down to her. Her heart seemed to lodge in her throat.

Oh my God, he's going to kiss me.

She melted against him, and all the while he placed his lips gently on her cheek before moving away from her.

She blinked, unsure of what exactly had happened.

She stepped back and bumped into her car, embarrassment filling her.

"I'll see you soon, Roxxy."

He ushered her into her car, and before Roxxy knew it, she was driving away.

She slowed to a halt at the red light of an intersection, still in shock. She reached up and pressed her fingers to the spot where his warm lips had touched.

"What the hell just happened?"

7

Myles chuckled, thinking back to earlier that day. He strolled around to where his team had been assembled. The recruits had already been dismissed, and the guys were just shooting shit, waiting for him to return from escorting her to her car.

He'd shut each one of them up once he confirmed that he had indeed asked Roxxy out for dinner and she'd accepted.

And they thought he would chicken out of asking a woman as beautiful as Roxxy out.

His teammates must not really know him.

He was Myles Fucking Burton.

And he loved women.

A horn blew behind him, breaking into his thoughts. He waved and pushed down on the gas pedal. In about fifteen minutes, he would be arriving at Roxxy's hotel.

The song on the radio changed to one of his favorite old-school tunes.

"I haven't heard this in a while," he said, turning the volume up. It was a song that his father played a thousand times. It had grown on Myles through the years.

Myles's father was a lover of all music. As a child, Myles couldn't think of a time his parents weren't blaring their favorites on their off days. Friday nights, especially, his parents put on their tunes and just danced together in the living room. The three Burton children, Myles, the oldest, his sister Shona who was two years behind him, and Clint, the youngest, gathered and watched their parents.

Jacob Burton twirled their mother, Jessica, around the living room, goofing off to get a laugh out of the kids.

As a child, Myles had rolled his eyes, but now as an adult, he could see that his parents were very much in love with each other.

Bobbing his head to the music, he chimed in, singing along with the chorus. "You are my lady. You're everything I need and more."

You are my lady.

You're all that I'm living for.

Myles snapped his fingers, strolling down memory

lane as the smooth voice of Freddie Jackson filled the air.

After arriving back at the precinct, he hadn't got the chance to speak with Roxxy again. She had been with her team members in one of the conference rooms combing through the police procedures handbooks.

But that hadn't stopped him. It was easy to find out which hotel Roxxy was staying at and even easier to get her cell phone number.

He'd sent her a text informing her what time he'd be picking her up.

Roxxy: How did you get my cell phone number?

Myles: I'm a cop. That's accessible information to dig up.

Roxxy: Hmmm.... I guess we're really going out?

Myles: I'm a man of my word. Wear something nice. I'll be there at seven-thirty.

Roxxy: What? That doesn't give me much time to get ready.

Myles: You can't fix perfection. See you soon.

Myles knew he was smooth in his reply, but he had to admit he was honest. Roxxy Sutton was a beautiful woman.

He was dressed in slacks and a dark button-down. The restaurant he was taking Roxxy to didn't require a tie, and he was thankful for that. The sun was just going down, and he had a great night planned for them.

Roxxy Sutton wouldn't know what hit her.

He grinned and turned onto the street her hotel was located on. The song was still playing, and he was still grooving to it. Mr. Jackson knew what he was talking about, and Myles was thankful his pops had introduced him to real music.

I love your shine
Shine, shine, shine.
Let's make it last.
Until the end of time.

The song was cut off by an incoming call. Myles glanced down at the touch screen on his dashboard and saw Ash's name.

"Yo," he answered, using his hands-free device.

"Yo, man," Ash responded. He and his friend had made up and were back on good terms. "You really going through with this?"

"I am." Myles laughed.

"I know the guys were pressuring you to do this, but you don't have to take her out if you don't want to." The joking faded from Ash's voice.

"I want to. Matter of fact, I've been thinking about her since the first time I saw her," Myles admitted honestly. He wouldn't share this with anyone but his close friend.

Ash was like a brother to him, and he knew that Ash wouldn't judge him. Myles had been there when Ash decided to finally take the next step with Deana. He was also there the night Ash saved her from an asshole trying to push up on her.

They were brothers in blue and would always have each other's backs.

"Wow. Never thought I'd hear this from you." Ash chuckled. "Has the mighty Myles met his match?"

"Shut up." Myles grinned. It would take one hell of a woman to tame him. Images of Roxxy's smile came to mind, and his breath escaped him as if something slammed into his abdomen. "I gotta go. I'm pulling up now."

"Have fun, and don't do anything I wouldn't do."

The line went dead before Myles could even respond with a snide remark.

Slowing his car, he turned into the parking lot and drove up to the front of the building. His gaze landed on a curvy figure waiting for him.

"Jesus," he murmured, his gaze meeting Roxxy's. He guided his vehicle to a stop and put it in park. He exited the car, his eyes greedily taking her in. Her white dress hung off her shoulder, revealing her bare skin. It clung to her frame and stopped mid-calf. Her feet were encased in heels that showed off her hot-pink-painted toenails. "Roxxy."

He was rendered speechless.

She was a knockout.

He didn't think it could happen, but she'd somehow improved perfection.

"Myles. How are you?" she asked with a small smile. Her hair cascaded down her back in dark waves. Her makeup was light, and her lips were stained his favorite color.

Red.

"I'm much better now that I'm in your presence." He held out a hand for her.

The young valet was openly checking out Roxxy's backside. His gaze met Myles's, who instantly narrowed his eyes on the kid. His face grew pale. He stumbled back and turned, quickly making his way inside the hotel. Myles smirked. Roxxy, unbeknownst to the silent altercation, placed her smaller in his and allowed him to walk her to his car.

"Smooth, Officer Burton." She laughed.

Myles's heart thudded at the spark in her eyes.

Turning to him, she paused them by the door. "I have to admit you are something else."

Myles grinned and glanced around. The doorman quickly averted his eyes. Myles bit back a snort.

"Myles. This is a business dinner, so I can ask you some questions about your job and procedures," she insisted.

He opened the door and helped her into the car.

"I don't recall labeling this a business dinner." He hastily shut the door at the sound of her sputtering.

No, Roxxy didn't know what was in store for her.

A night with Myles Burton would be a night she'd never forget.

What have I gotten myself into?

Roxxy tried to steady her rapid heartbeat. Myles Burton dressed the way he was and smelling all good had her squeezing her thighs shut.

There was nothing better than a sexy man with a good cologne. She just wanted to bury her face into his chest and breath in his scent.

The restaurant he'd taken her to was phenomenal. She couldn't put her fork down. The atmosphere was comfortable, and there was a small band wooing the patrons while they ate their dinner.

"I'm glad you're enjoying yourself," Myles remarked, staring at her over the candlelit table.

The ambiance of the establishment was definitely romantic. No matter how many times she'd tried to ask him questions, he'd give a short answer and flip the conversation to something else.

"I am." She smiled sheepishly. Setting her fork

down on the table, she reached for her wine glass and took another sip. "Now getting back to what I was trying to ask. Don't think I haven't noticed you avoiding my questions."

His lips curled up into a crooked grin. He snagged his glass and toyed with it. Roxxy's attention dropped down to his long fingers, and she gulped.

Her gaze flew back up to his. She dared not go down the pathway of thoughts.

"I'm sure you've read plenty of procedure manuals while at the precinct. My team and I are very by-the-book." He lifted his glass and downed the rest of the contents.

"Is that so?" She took the time to openly study him. Her fingers begged to trail over his bald head. She wanted to feel his beard against her skin. She leaned forward and rested her elbow on the table. "So you're telling me that no matter what, you and your men don't ever take matters into your own hands and do things your way?"

He paused, the smile disappearing from his lips.

A dark veil appeared in his eyes.

"We do what must be done." The playfulness was gone from him.

He was a large man who knew how to handle a gun, and she was sure he would know how to handle her.

A shiver slid down Roxxy's spine.

There was a dark, haunting side of Myles that she wouldn't ever want to be on the receiving end of. There was a reason his team was one of the best in the state. Each man was a decorated member of the Columbia Police Department.

But there was something about Myles.

The music changed into an upbeat tempo. Roxxy broke Myles's gaze and spun away. A few couples were laughing while dancing.

Roxxy swiveled her gaze back to Myles with raised eyebrows and tipped her head toward the dance floor.

She hadn't meant for their conversation to sour.

It was time to turn it around.

"What?" He took in the people swaying to the beat and shook his head. "Oh, no. I don't dance."

"Really?" She pushed her chair back. She grabbed the napkin from her lap and tossed it on the table.

Roxxy didn't know where this bravery was coming from.

Maybe it was the wine.

Or it had just been so long since she'd had the attention of a man, and her body was telling her it was time.

She stood and sashayed a few steps from the table with a little extra sway in her hips. She glanced over her shoulder at Myles. He didn't try to hide the fact he had got caught staring at her ass.

"Well, Officer Burton. You can sit here if you want to. But there is something that must get done tonight." She tossed him a wink and spun around.

The sound of another chair scraping the floor gave her pause.

She had him.

A figure pressed close behind her.

Myles.

"I have a better idea," he murmured, his lips ghosting over her ear.

Her body trembled at the feel of him pressing against her. Everyone else faded away.

At the moment, it was just the two of them.

"What?" she breathed.

His steady hand circled her wrist. He gently twirled her around to face him. She stared up at him, waiting. His hand came up to touch her bottom lip. His eyes darkened as they focused on her mouth.

"Come with me," he whispered.

She didn't know where, but she found herself nodding.

He took her hand and led her around the dance floor. His hand on her was comforting. They walked through the restaurant and stepped out of a set of

French doors. The smell of the nighttime air filled her nostrils.

"Oh my," she gasped, taking in her surroundings.

There was a long pier off the building that overlooked the river. Soft white lights twinkled on the railing, providing a little light.

At the moment, it was just the two of them. The music floated through the open windows. It was faint, and the new song was one that had a slow tempo and was romantic.

"It's beautiful, isn't it?" He pulled her closer to him, tucking her into his side.

"It is," she agreed. It was a magnificent sight to behold. The river flowed before them, and Roxxy breathed in the scent around them.

They stopped at the edge of the pier without a word.

Roxxy leaned against the railing and took in the sight of the river at night.

Myles slipped behind her and trapped her. He bent down and pushed his face into the crook of her neck. He nuzzled it, and her head fell to the side to grant him permission.

He closed the gap between them, and her heart raced at the feeling of something hard resting on her ass.

"I think this is much better than me embarrassing

myself in there trying to dance." His lips brushed her ear.

"I don't know," she teased. "It would have been hilarious to see you dance." She squealed as his hand came up and tickled her side. She broke his hold on her and turned around to face him.

His hooded eyes were locked on her.

"What are we doing, Myles?" she whispered.

She had to be going crazy.

She was seriously considering inviting him back to her hotel.

He leaned closer to her, and her heart thundered. His hand rested on the small of her back and brought her flush against him.

"We are enjoying each other's company," he answered.

She slid her hands up his hard chest and bit back a groan at the size, strength, and power of the man holding her as if she were a delicate flower. He made her feel safe and protected. Her hand continued up to the back of his neck, and she guided his head down to her.

Tomorrow she'd blame her actions on the excellent food, wine, and fresh air.

She wanted Myles Burton.

His lips covered hers, and she was lost.

Myles drove his tongue inside her mouth,

commanding the kiss. She pushed closer to him, a moan slipping from her. She tightened her hands around his neck. She refused to budge.

God, he can kiss.

She tore her lips from his. Both of them were left breathing hard. Her core clenched from the heat in his gaze.

"Want to go get a nightcap at my hotel?" It was her chicken way of asking him to take her back and ravish her.

Her body was going haywire at the moment, and she needed Myles to soothe the ache between her legs.

His hand came up and cupped her face. He pressed a hard kiss to her lips. "Let's get out of here."

8

Myles sensed Roxxy's nervousness. He could tell it had taken a lot for her to drum up the nerve to ask him back to her hotel. That was why he'd tried to make her feel comfortable in the car once they'd left the restaurant. He got her laughing at his jokes, even played music trivia.

Hell, he had to find a way to calm himself down.

His cock had been trying to drill a hole in his slacks to break free. The feeling of Roxxy's curvy body was enough to almost make him blow his fucking load before they'd even got started.

Now in the elevator, he couldn't take his eyes off her. Her light-brown skin begged for his touch. Her bare shoulders were downright sexy. He never really knew when he'd got into shoulders, but Roxxy's were perfect.

"Why are you staring at me?" she asked softly, her voice breaking into his thoughts.

"Because I think you are beautiful," he replied automatically.

"You're just saying that." Her lips turned up into the corners, and she looked away.

He snagged her small wrist and tugged her close to him. Everything about her was dainty compared to him, but he knew she was much tougher than she appeared.

She stumbled into him with a gasp. He wrapped an arm around her and slid his hand down to her hip.

"I say what's on my mind. I don't have any reason to lie." He stared down into her eyes while she leaned into him.

Her eyes widened when he pressed his lower half against her. He wanted to make it very clear, tonight, she was his.

He glanced up and saw they had a few more flights before they arrived at her floor.

"Can I come clean about something?" She bit her bottom lip with a guilty expression on her face.

Myles's raised an eyebrow and nodded.

She blew out a deep breath and reached up to dust something off his shirt. "I wasn't really inviting you here for a nightcap."

The elevator announced her floor, and the doors opened. She stepped out of the car. His gaze dropped down to her ass, and his mind was flooded with all the things he could possibly do with it.

"I'm shocked." He placed his hand on his chest and followed behind her into the hallway. "And here I thought we would enjoy a nice drink or something."

He closed the distance between them and tipped her chin up so he could look into her eyes.

"Well, you're going to be sorely disappointed because there is not an ounce of alcohol in my room."

Myles chuckled. His thumb ran across her bottom lip. "Don't worry. Alcohol is the last thing on my mind. There's something else I'm wanting."

"What is that?" she whispered.

"Take me to your room—unless you really want me to show you out here in this hall." He bent down and softly kissed her lips. He didn't have a problem with pushing her up to the wall and sinking inside her. He couldn't care less who saw them.

She swallowed hard and turned away. Myles strolled behind her, enjoying the sway of her hips. The material clung to her, showcasing her wide hips, and he wanted to thank the designer for their gift in dressmaking.

She paused outside a door and pulled her keycard from her purse. She spun around and leaned back against the door.

"What's wrong?" He placed one hand on the door, trapping Roxxy between it and him.

"I've never really done this before," she admitted.

"Done what?" He paused. Was Roxxy about to say she was a virgin? His heart pulsed double time, and panic set in.

"A one-night stand," she blurted.

Relief filled him that she didn't say she was a virgin. He could deal with the fact that she'd never had a one-night stand. She didn't look the type. He'd had plenty in his past that he could barely remember, but Roxxy was definitely someone he would be remembering.

He took the card from her and leaned down where his lips brushed hers. "Do you want me, Roxxy?"

"God, yes," she breathed.

Unable to resist, he covered her mouth with his. The taste of her was addictive. He caught a faint hint of her wine and dinner mint she'd eaten. Pulling her away from the door, he refused to break the kiss. He fumbled at first before successfully sliding the card into the slot.

He nudged the door open with his foot. He reached down and lifted Roxxy by the back of her knees with one hand. Her hands slid over his bald head, sending a shiver down his spine.

He stalked into the room and kicked the door shut.

Breaking the kiss, Myles glanced around the suite. A lamp was left on. Its soft rays illuminated the corner of the sitting area. It was a lovely suite, but all Myles cared about was the bedroom.

"I'm too heavy, Myles. Put me down." She giggled, wrapping her arms around his neck.

The scent of her perfume filled his senses, and he had one thing on his mind.

"What are you talking about?" he asked gruffly. She barely weighed anything. He benched more than her. He gave her ass one good squeeze and headed toward the bedroom.

"Never mind," she breathed. Her lips brushed his cheek, trailing kisses on his face.

A growl slipped from his chest.

"Hurry."

Myles strode into the room and paused near the bed. His heart raced as he breathed in Roxxy's scent. Her body writhed against his. He didn't really want to sit Roxxy down, but he had no choice. She slid along his front until her feet were on the floor. They paused, staring at each other in the low light.

Myles glanced around and took in the lamp on the nightstand by the bed. He turned it on, not wanting to miss one inch of Roxxy's body. Myles pulled his wallet out of his pants and tossed on the table. He moved toward her and reached for her.

He cupped her cheeks and lowered his head to hers. He covered her mouth with his. Her lips parted, welcoming his tongue inside. Her taste was one he couldn't get enough of. The sounds of her moans fueled his desire for her.

He tore his lips from hers and pressed hot kisses to her neck. "How do we get you out of this?" he bit out.

"There's a zipper in the back." She gasped, pushing near him.

Myles made quick work of removing it from her. She stood before him in a strapless bra and lace panties. The sight of Roxxy almost brought him to his knees.

A coy smile played on her lips.

"Like what you see?" she teased, turning around in place. She looked over her shoulder at Myles.

His gaze slowly roamed her soft brown skin.

Oh, yeah.

He did.

Closing the gap between them, he gripped her hair in his hand and tugged her back to him. He pressed himself against her. A gasp escaped her lips.

"What do you think?" she asked playfully.

He placed a soft kiss to her shoulder while undoing the clasp of her bra. It fell to the floor, with neither of them paying any attention to it. Myles moved her hair to angle her neck to give him full access to it. He bathed her skin with his tongue while he reached around Roxxy with his free hand to cup her voluptuous mounds.

"Perfection."

A groan released from Myles at the sensation of her beaded nipples in his hands. He teased her, pulling on her nipples but then soothing them with a gentle stroke of his hands.

"Myles," Roxxy moaned, leaning her full weight on him.

Her hair was entwined around his fingers. He used it as an anchor to hold her in place.

"I like the sound of my name on your lips," he muttered. He slid his free hand along her abdomen, and it disappeared underneath her panties. "Tell me what you want."

He parted her folds and was met with the evidence of her arousal. Her gasps grew louder while he gently rubbed his finger across her swollen nub.

He grew harder, imagining her slick sheath enclosing his cock.

He needed to be inside her.

Now.

Roxxy couldn't breathe.

She couldn't move.

Myles's fingers were driving her toward that sweet spot of oblivion.

Her body was frozen in place while Myles took control of her. His fingers strummed her.

"I'm waiting," he rasped in her ear.

She turned around in his arms and stared up at him. His dark-eyed gaze traveled the length of her, and the pleased expression on his face made her feel like a sexy siren.

It made her feel as if she were the only girl in the world.

"You," she whispered.

He leaned down and pressed a hard kiss to her lips. Roxxy began undoing the buttons of his shirt. Their mouths molded together. His tongue slid inside her mouth, dominating the kiss.

Their movements grew frantic as they discarded his clothes until he was left in just his boxer briefs.

She had been dying to see him in all his glory, and her breath escaped her. "Jesus."

The hard planes of his chest were well defined. His dark skin was smooth and looked as if an artist had painted every ridge and muscle. Her gaze dropped down to the large bulge hidden beneath the black cotton material covering him.

She swallowed hard.

Oh my.

"Take your panties off, Roxxy."

Her eyes flew back up to his. The heat of his stare alone had her reaching for the material hugging her hips.

"Take your boxers off." She raised an eyebrow. If she had to reveal her full self to him, he needed to do the same in return.

He barked a laugh. "Very well."

She couldn't take her eyes off him if she tried. He stripped the offending item off. His long length sprang free, and her knees grew weak.

She licked her lips.

Wow.

Everything about Myles Burton was large.

An ache began in deep in her core.

A growl ripped through the air. "Come here."

He snatched her close, pressing her body against his while he lowered his head and covered her mouth with his in a hard, brutal kiss.

They fell back onto the bed.

Her legs automatically parted, allowing him to settle between the valley of her thighs.

Roxxy ran her hand over Myles's bald head. She was fascinated by it.

Myles smoothed his hands on her body and shifted lower, breaking their kiss. She gasped at the feel of him taking her breast inside his hot mouth. His fingers trailed her thighs before connecting with her clit again.

Her body arched off the bed.

He nipped her bud with his teeth, and a cry erupted from her lips.

"Myles," she whimpered, unable to complete a sentence in her current state. Her legs widened for him. She felt wanton and abandoned all her inhibitions and opened herself for him.

He pushed his finger inside her and paused.

"You're so fucking wet," he muttered against her mound. He withdrew then pushed inside again, this time adding another finger.

She moaned from the invasion. Myles stroked her, stretching her channel. Her body was strung tight, making her feel things she'd never experienced before.

Roxxy pulled his head up and fused her lips to his. A thick hardness pressed on her leg.

He continued to thrust his fingers inside her, but she wanted more.

She needed more.

The ache inside her core grew, and it would only be satisfied by Myles's cock.

His thumb brushed her clit, and she practically exploded.

"Stop teasing me," she cried out.

A wolfish grin spread across his face. An arrogant glint appeared in his eyes, revealing he knew precisely what he had been doing to Roxxy.

He continued to fuck her with his fingers, shunting her toward the edge of her orgasm.

He was playing unfair.

How dare he ensure she took pleasure from him?

"You don't like this?" he quietly asked. He leaned down and ran his tongue over her nipple. He pushed his fingers inside her, harder.

She rotated her hips and met each of his thrusts.

"God, yes."

"Myles will do." He chuckled, scraping his teeth across her hard bud.

Son of a bitch has the nerve to be cocky.

A sheen of sweat coated her skin. Unable to hold Myles's gaze, she closed her eyes tight. She was close to climaxing, and if she continued to stare into his dark pools, she'd be a goner.

Never had a lover taken the time to wring such pleasure from her.

Not Korey.

No other man before him.

Myles was dangerous.

"Please." The word slipped from her lips in a deep guttural groan.

"Yes, ma'am." His response was raw but quiet.

He withdrew his fingers, and she almost begged for him to put them back.

He leaned over to the edge of the bed for a brief moment. The crinkle of a foil packet being opened was the only sound.

She felt so vulnerable and open. Her body trembled with anticipation of what was to come.

She opened her eyes to find him braced above her.

He propped her one leg over his arm, opening her fully to him. His lower body shifted, and something broad and blunt probed her folds.

A whimper escaped her.

One swift thrust, and he was deep inside her.

They both cried out together.

"Myles."

"Roxxy."

He paused at first, allowing her to get used to his invasion. Her muscles contracted around him, stretching to accommodate. There was a slight burning sensation, but she welcomed it.

Myles took control of her and their lovemaking.

She didn't have any issues with turning herself over to him.

He fucked her hard, giving her everything she needed.

He was every bit the alpha male.

He consumed her.

Breathed new life into her.

Her whimpers filled the air. She couldn't hold back if she tried. Myles was so deep, and the tip of his cock brushed her most sensitive areas.

He flipped them over, and she suddenly found herself on top of him.

Her eyes flew open. She gazed down at Myles, and their eyes connected. No words were needed. She instantly rose and impaled herself onto his hard length.

She moved faster, riding her big strong lover.

His eyes fluttered closed, and she felt empowered. His hands rested on her hips, guiding her.

His groans grew louder.

Breathless and feeling the tell-tale signs of her orgasm coming for her, she rested her hands on the bed and turned herself over to taking pleasure from Myles.

She ground her hips down on him. His grip on her skin grew tighter while they worked together.

He thrust up, pulling her down on him harder and faster.

A shudder rippled its way through her body as she reached her climax. She squeezed her eyes shut tight, crying out through her release.

It was the most intense orgasm she'd ever had. Every muscle in her body grew taut, and she rode the waves of pleasure.

A low growl erupted from Myles. He wrapped his arms around her and flipped them back over, thrusting harder and harder until he finally came.

"Ahh..." he cried out.

She cradled him to her, wrapping her arms around him. He rolled them over onto their sides, keeping her close to him. She nuzzled her face into the crook of his neck.

She refused to think of the morning, or him leaving.

No, she was going to bask in the afterglow of the best sex of her life.

Snuggling against his hard body, she drifted off to sleep.

9

Myles glanced down at Roxxy and couldn't explain what he was feeling. Generally, after sex, he'd leave. Most women knew what they signed up for, so it was never a big deal when the time came for him to go.

But not this time.

He wanted to watch Roxxy wake up.

He was mesmerized by her beauty.

They'd had sex—no, made love twice.

She felt perfect lying next to him. Her soft naked curves fit him as if she were made for him. He pulled her closer, loving the feeling of her breasts pushed up against his side.

He glanced over at the clock on the nightstand, finding it to be a little after five in the morning.

He would have to leave soon.

But he couldn't get his body to move away from Roxxy.

Memories of the way her body responded to his

would be etched into his mind forever. The look on her face as she'd reached her climaxes brought on a stirring beneath the covers.

Fuck.

He wanted her again.

He should let her sleep, but he didn't always listen to the voice of reason.

Her soft snore filled the air. Myles brushed her hair from her forehead and laid a kiss on it. He left a trail of kisses on her cheeks and lips.

Her mouth curved into a beautiful smile.

"Again?" Her husky voice went straight to his dick. It stood to attention fully engorged and ready to go.

"It appears I can't get enough of you," he murmured.

Roxxy's eyes opened, and his breath was ripped from his lungs. She sat up and rested on her elbow and stared back at him.

Her hair was tousled and flowed around her shoulders. She looked as if she'd been royally fucked, and pride filled Myles's chest.

I did that.

The sheet fell away from her body, revealing her large breasts. Myles had become intimately familiar with them. Her dark-brown nipples were beaded into tight buds. He licked his lips, remembering the taste and feel of them in his mouth.

"Well, let me see what I can do for you." A playful glint appeared in her eyes. She pushed him back onto the bed.

He fell back with a chuckle as she leaned over him.

How the fuck did he get so lucky? She hadn't complained once and had been eager every time they'd fucked.

She covered his lips with hers. He threaded his fingers into her dark hair and took over the kiss. He thrust his tongue forward, sweeping into her mouth.

Her breasts rested on his chest, and a growl escaped him. He slid his hand down her body and settled it on the small of her back.

She tore her lips away from his and pressed kisses on his chin, then chest, and continued to go lower.

"You do whatever you like," he grunted.

Roxxy tossed him a wink and continued her journey lower. Her tongue traveled down the hard plains of his abdomen. If he didn't know any better, she counted each one.

She moved the blanket out of the way, allowing his cock to spring free.

"Looks like someone wants attention." She smiled and shifted to kneel between his legs.

Her focus was on his dick, and Myles had a hard time catching his breath while watching her.

Her small hand wrapped around his rigid length, and he was unable to formulate words.

She stroked his length before leaning down and licking the tip with her tongue.

His heart palpitated.

Shit.

He couldn't take his eyes off the sight of his cock disappearing between her lips.

Roxxy's eyes fluttered shut with a moan slipping from her.

Myles grew tense. Her warm mouth felt so fucking good.

He was in Heaven.

She pulled back then slipped him farther inside.

"Yes," he hissed, gripping her hair and guiding himself inside her mouth.

Her hand clung to the base of him tight while she sucked and licked his entire length.

His eyes closed, and he basked in the feel of her sucking him off. He allowed her to take control.

Her hand moved up and down in tandem with her mouth.

"Fuck." His balls drew up tight, and he refused to blow that quick.

Not without her.

Myles always believed in making sure his lovers

reached their climax with him. He was a generous lover and didn't believe in being selfish.

"Roxxy," he called her.

She added her other hand, and he let out a curse. Her hands slid along him while she swallowed as much as she could.

"Shit. I don't want to release yet. Come here."

She paused and glanced up at him. He almost lost it at the sight of his dick in her mouth and her wide eyes staring at him. He felt her swallow, and he instantly had to withdraw from her mouth.

"What did I do?" she asked, lips glistening. She sat back with a little pout.

Jesus, she was the perfect woman. Her curvy frame was soft in all the right places, and her pussy took his cock with no complaints. He was a large man, and she hadn't complained, not once. They didn't have enough time to do all the freaky shit he could think of, but there was one thing he wanted.

"Shit. Everything. Your mouth is fucking perfect, but I can't come yet." He gripped her by her arm and pulled. He needed taste her. He didn't care if he was late to the station, he wanted Roxxy's sweet honey on his tongue.

"Then why'd you stop me?" She giggled, tucking her thick hair behind an ear.

"Because I want you to sit on my face."

"What?" Her voice grew breathless. She paused next to him with wide eyes.

He grinned. He wanted what he wanted. "You heard me. You. On my face. Now."

Roxxy suddenly grew shy.

Did he just say what I think he said?

She swallowed hard.

Her skin tingled at the intensity of his stare. Her core pulsated with the thought of what he was asking for.

"Myles—"

"Do you trust me, Roxxy?"

His deep baritone sent a shiver coursing through her body.

Wordlessly, she nodded.

How the hell could she not? After the night they'd had, she'd be a fool to deny him anything.

She pushed off the bed and knelt beside him while he shoved his pillows off onto the floor. He grinned, and her cheeks warmed.

The things she'd done with him had her face burning. The memories of their night together would be forever ingrained into her mind.

Myles helped guide her over him. Her legs spread apart, putting her center over his face.

She was utterly vulnerable.

Exposed.

Turned on.

Roxxy gripped the headboard, trying to find something to hold on to.

She glanced down, and her heart lost a beat.

"Don't go shy on me now." He chuckled.

A nervous giggle escaped Roxxy.

All laughter faded the second his lips closed around her clit.

She gasped.

His large hands cupped her ass, positioning her just where he wanted her.

Myles took his time kissing her in the most intimate of ways. His tongue slid through her silken folds, sending a tremor through her body.

A moan slipped from her as she gazed down at the man beneath her.

He devoured her.

She cried out her pleasure.

He made his way back to her clit and suckled it harder.

"Myles..." Her voice grew hoarse. Her hand flew from the headboard to his head. She didn't know what to hold on to, she just knew that she'd better buckle up for this ride.

Her back arched as her hips moved.

Her gaze made its way back down to Myles, taking in his closed eyes.

Her breaths came faster, making it harder for her to take in air.

His eyes opened, and he returned her stare. She could feel her orgasm coming for her.

Again?

Three in one night.

That was a new record for her.

"Don't hold back," Myles growled.

He latched on to her bud and continued his sweet torture.

She was floating high amongst the stars and clouds in the sky.

The first wave of her release floated over her. She cried out from the depths of her soul. The intensity of the climax grew. Her body shook as it consumed her.

Myles was there to catch all of her release.

He somehow shifted them, and she found herself on her stomach with her ass in the air.

She blinked, and Myles had entered her with one hard thrust from behind.

She braced her hands on the bed and met him stroke for stroke.

"Ahh..." she cried out.

Myles's hands found their way to her hair. He gripped it tight, anchoring her to him as his hips thrust harder and faster.

He fucked her relentlessly, taking everything from her.

She'd thought it before, but now she knew it.

One night with Myles just wouldn't be enough.

She was officially addicted.

10

"Officer Stowe was patrolling the area when she heard shots being fired," Mac announced to the group.

It was mid-morning, and SWAT was out on a call. A hostage situation involving a man and two unknown victims.

"According to Stowe, she drove around and witnessed a man standing in the street with a rifle. He then proceeded to enter that home and has barricaded himself in there."

This was a dangerous situation.

Myles glanced around and took in the street. People were milling about on the corner. Whenever there was a situation, there was a crowd.

"Stowe also reported that the rifle looked military grade."

"Shit," Myles muttered. With a high-powered rifle and the suspect probably hopped up on some type of drug, this made this mission even more precarious.

"We need all the civilians out of sight," Declan snapped, walking away from the BEAR. He stalked toward the patrol car and hollered a few orders.

Uniforms scrambled to do as he bid.

Myles turned back and tried to listen to his sergeant as best as he could, but thoughts of Roxxy crept into his mind. It had been two days since he'd left her hotel room.

The sounds of her moans still echoed in his mind.

He couldn't shake her.

It was to be one night of fun, but instead, he wanted another one.

To save her the awkward morning after, he'd slipped from her suite before she woke up. If he hadn't, he probably would have locked them away and kept her in the bed for a full twenty-four hours.

If he closed his eyes, he could still taste her.

"Barton!" Mac barked.

Myles blinked.

"Yeah." He cleared his throat. He looked around and found all eyes were on him.

Zain and Iker both had smirks on their damn faces. Brodie cocked an eyebrow at him.

Shit.

Now was not the time to be off in la-la land. They were about to go into a dangerous situation, and he needed to be fully aware of everything.

Mac gave him a hard stare before continuing on. "Ash was able to get the suspect on the telephone once, and he confirmed there are two hostages inside with him. The suspect would not verify if they were unharmed. The call was disconnected, and now he will not answer. The power company is here and will be cutting all power to the house."

Myles gave the nod to show he was listening. This tactic was used to isolate the suspect. No television, radio, or any other way he could get information on what was going on outside. The local news channels were posted outside the police tape, all reporting what was going on. It would do them more damage than good if the suspect could see and know what they were doing.

"Why the hell they let those civilians get so damn close?" Declan rejoined the group. "They had one job to do."

Myles agreed with Declan. The last thing they needed was the suspect opening fire on the nosey people trying to see what was going on.

"What's the move?" Myles tried to keep Roxxy from creeping back into his thoughts.

"Since we don't know the status of the hostages, we're going to have been careful with this. I want you, Brodie, Iker, and Zain to approach the house. Once the power is cut, we're going to provide a cell phone. This should make him open a line of communication with us. If that fails, then we'll breach the home."

Myles nodded and glanced over at his teammates. They'd practiced this plenty of times. SWAT always didn't rush into situations with guns blazing. When it came to rescuing hostages, they had to be delicate about the mission. Not knowing if the hostages were harmed or safe heightened the tension. The ultimate goal of a case like this would be to extract everyone from the house unscathed.

Myles followed Brodie over to the other side of the BEAR, where they could obtain what would be needed.

"Same as always." Brodie opened a compartment on the vehicle.

"Yeah," Myles responded.

Brodie would be first in their procession line. He'd carry the shield to protect them from random shots that could be taken at them. The next person would have the tool to break the glass and insert the device into the home while the other two behind provided cover.

It was standard procedure, but having an armed suspect who could decide to use them as target practice made this extremely dangerous.

"Just as we practiced. In and out quick," Zain agreed.

He and Iker came to stand next to Myles. They

both had their weapons in their hands. Myles didn't doubt for a second these two would protect him and Brodie. He was close to each member, and there wasn't anything they wouldn't do for each other.

"I just need Myles to stop daydreaming. Don't think you got away from telling us what happened with you and the surveyor chick." Iker chuckled. "Beers on me tonight."

Myles rolled his eyes. He pulled his mask up over his face and secured his helmet. "One day, boys, when you grow up, you'll learn not to kiss and tell."

"Hmm...kissing was involved. Now we have to hear what happened." Zain barked a hearty laugh. "We all live through your sexcapades."

"Speak for yourself. I get plenty of women," Iker said.

"Why haven't I seen any of these so-called women?" Zain scratched his head.

"Because I wouldn't want to scare them off with your ugly mug of a face," Iker replied.

Myles and Brodie chuckled at the two of them.

Myles glanced over and caught a glare from Mac, who was speaking with the other sergeants in charge of the scene. "We best get a move on it."

"Here is the cell you are to insert into the window." Declan joined them. He handed the cheap phone to Myles. "Ash is staying behind to try to talk the suspect down. Mac and I will be posted to provide additional cover. We don't like how many windows are in the house. We can't see him and don't want to take any chances."

"The power?" Zain asked.

All amusement and joking had been put to the side.

"It's been cut. You're good to go. Be careful and keep your eyes open." Declan met their eyes and gave the nod. He turned and jogged over where Mac was waiting for him.

"Let's roll, men," Myles announced, motioning to Iker and Zain.

Ash had plenty of experience negotiating. He was a natural at it and had an excellent track record. Myles trusted his close friend to be able to convince the man to release the hostages.

They lined up in close formation and approached the house. It was daylight, and everything in the yard was visible. Myles was thankful for the sun. Had this been at night, it would make it harder for all the unknowns who would be hidden under cover of darkness.

They kept a tight line with Brodie in front. Iker and Zain had their weapons trained on the house.

Silence ensued.

Tensions were high.

This was not a practice drill.

It was the real deal.

Myles could feel Iker behind him. They arrived at the side of the front porch and stayed as close to the home as possible. They slowly walked to the first window. Myles held the long metal pole with a clamp at the end. He'd use it to break the glass and toss the phone inside.

Brodie raised his fist, signaling their arrival at the destination.

The older home had outdated windows. It would be simple to hit the pane and smash it. From experience, the newer homes came fitted with glass that could withstand more pressure and were harder to shatter.

Myles moved in closer, staying conscious of his surroundings. He extended the pole with the hammer edge toward the target. Ready, he waited for the signal.

"We're good," Iker murmured quietly.

Myles swung the hammer, fracturing the glass. He tossed the phone inside.

Mission accomplished.

A man's deep voice cursed from inside.

"Move," Brodie snapped.

They immediately backed away from the structure. Myles kept his eyes on the house, praying the guy didn't come to the window and start shooting.

It seemed like hours, but only minutes had passed since they'd completed their mission. They got back at the BEAR, unharmed.

"Good job, men." Mac and Declan arrived where they stood. Their department-issue semiautomatic rifles hung from around their necks. Had the suspect opened fire, he would have paid dearly for it.

Now he was away from the house, Myles allowed his body to relax. He glanced at his team and nodded.

"We're going to see if Ash can reach him. If we can't talk him out of the building then we'll breach the perimeter and enter," Declan informed them.

"Sergeant MacArthur!" a voice called out.

Myles turned and saw a woman in uniform walking over to them. She was an African-American with dark braids pulled back into a ponytail.

"Officer Stowe," Mac replied, facing her.

She stopped before them and motioned over to the street corner where another patrol officer was speaking with a few women.

"Those ladies over there came down here because they know who is in the house," she said, rotating back to them.

She was calm, and Myles could see the wisdom and experience in her eyes. This was one beat cop who didn't take no shit.

"They were watching the television and caught the news reports. They can identify the suspect."

Good. All the cops had was his description but no name. He'd refused to give up a name from what Myles knew.

"Iker and Zain, escort them over to the command van. We don't know the mindset of the suspect and don't want him randomly shooting," Mac ordered.

"Yes, sir." Iker and Zain left with Officer Stowe.

"We're giving this fucker one time to come out. This has been drawn out longer than necessary," Declan announced.

"I agree. The longer we let him remain in there, the more he could escalate," Myles said.

He glanced back at the house from around the edge of the BEAR.

This was the part of being a SWAT officer he hated the most.

Waiting.

Myles was growing restless with the waiting. They'd received an update that Ash had made contact with the suspect. Apparently, his name was Darius Sherman, and he had a mental history. According to his sisters, Lisa and Kim, he was diagnosed with paranoid schizophrenia and was off his medications. The house belonged to an ex-girlfriend of his who now lived with her new girlfriend.

"Mr. Sherman would not allow Ash to speak to the two women. We're going to go in prepared to meet the worst."

The team surrounded Mac while he gave instructions.

SWAT would do what they did best.

It was unfortunate that they had to assume the worst, and the suspect was not cooperating.

If he was indeed off of his mediations and a paranoid schizo, then there was no telling where he was mentally.

"We're going to use a normal hostage extraction protocol. The front door will be the entry point. A few patrols will post up in the back to make sure he doesn't try to escape through the rear door."

Myles listened to the instructions of his sergeant. These were vital. Following orders was how they proved to be a successful team. They worked well together, and each trusted Mac to lead. Each man would be reviewing protocols and knew exactly what would need to be done.

Around him stood the men he knew would do their damnedest to ensure the hostages would be removed safely.

"Any questions?" Mac asked.

Face masks and helmets were pulled into place.

Myles willed his heart to slow down. Anxiety and nerves didn't belong out in the field. He breathed in deeply and drew his semiautomatic weapon closer to his body as he waited for the phrase he knew were coming.

"SWAT, let's hunt." Mac's voice rung out clear and concise.

Three little words put everyone in the mindset that it was time to do what they did best.

The team moved with their practiced precision. They worked together like a well-oiled machine.

Brodie arrived at the door first with his shield in place. Zain came from behind with the battering ram. Two good hits, and the wood splintered.

"CPD!" Declan's hard voice shot through the air.

They entered the building swiftly in a single-file line with their weapons drawn. Iker and Myles were the first inside.

"Clear," Iker called out, scoping his side of the room.

"Clear," Myles echoed, his gaze sweeping the living room.

The rest of the team moved on, trusting Myles and Iker. Myles and Iker would fall back to the end of the line as they walked through the house.

"Hands on your head!" Mac shouted from the back room.

Myles braced for the sound of gunfire, but it never came. He watched Declan and Brodie go into the small room.

"Hostages. Where are they?" Declan asked.

Myles motioned for Iker and Zain to follow him without waiting to hear the answer. They still had to secure the rest of the house. They could never be too careful when in a hot situation. Even though they knew it was the two women and Darius, they had to be sure there was no one else in the house.

They continued on.

Dining room—cleared.

Kitchen—nothing.

They headed up the stairs.

Myles pushed open the first door, finding it to be a little bathroom. "Clear," he shouted.

"Clear," Zain called out, stepping from his area.

"Shit," Iker cursed. He disappeared into the last room.

Myles and Zain paused in the doorway where Iker was.

The two women were sprawled on the large bed. The dark-haired one's eyes were open and lifeless, staring at the ceiling. Blood caked the sheets and their bodies. Bullet holes lined the walls, and casings were left on the floor.

It had been a massacre.

There was no telling how long they'd been there. From the looks of it, Darius had caught them in the bed and sprayed them with bullets.

"Anything?" Myles asked, but he already knew the answer.

Iker checked for a pulse on both of them and stepped back, shaking his head.

They were too late.

"We found the hostages," Myles announced through their communicators. "Call for the medical examiner."

11

Roxxy had to force herself to concentrate on the meeting at hand. Their team was currently reviewing over the details of the audit and what was still needed in order for them to conclude. Her gaze roamed around the conference table and took in their team. Each of the men were loyal to the company and had worked for her father for years.

Images of Myles kept creeping into her thoughts. She had to force them from her mind. No matter how much she wanted to replay their night together, now was not the time.

"SWAT is out on a call now. When they return, we will follow up with them and finish the interviews," Earl stated.

Roxxy blinked.

Candidate interviews.

She could do that.

"I've already spoken with Sergeants MacArthur,

Owen, and Officer Burton," she remarked, looking down at her notes.

"Oh? When did you meet with Burton?" her father asked. He paused rifling through his papers and lifted his head.

Her face warmed at his innocent question. "Right after the tryouts."

Earl eyed her before giving her a slight nod.

She blew out a deep breath, thankful he didn't question her further.

"They've been dispatched on call for hours. I think we should go out there," Phil suggested. He was one of the top auditors with the company. He, too, was a former cop who after taking a bullet to the knee, decided on using his skills in a different manner. He had never been cleared to work in the field again and did not want to spend the rest of his career behind a desk. Logistics Intelligence Services gave former policemen and women a way to use the skills they had developed over the years.

"Great idea. Why don't you and Roxxy head out and observe." Earl motioned to them.

Roxxy glanced at her co-worker and offered a tight smile. "Lou and Jim can handle the interviews. I want the men and women who tried out for SWAT to be included."

"Yes, sir," Lou and Jim echoed.

"We should be concluding within the next day or so," Earl announced.

Even though Roxxy knew they wouldn't be in Columbia for a long time, her father's words still hit her like cold water to the face. She'd go back to her small town while Myles would still be here.

They hadn't promised each other anything. She knew when she'd invited him up to her hotel that it was going to be for a night of hot sex.

Myles certainly hadn't let her down.

Hell, he had her aching now just with the memories of everything they'd done.

"Ready to go?" Phil's voice broke through her thoughts.

Roxxy glanced around and saw her team had dispersed. Earl stood at the door eyeing her.

"Sorry. Yeah, I'm ready." She gathered her papers and put them in her binder. She stood from the table, embarrassed at being caught in a daydream.

They walked to the doorway together, but he held up a hand to her.

"I'll go grab my car and pull it around." Phil must have sensed the boss wanted to have a private moment with her.

"Okay. Thanks." Roxxy tucked her dark hair behind her ear.

He disappeared from the room. Earl closed the door behind him.

Roxxy swallowed hard and held her binder close to her chest. She suddenly felt sixteen again, staring up at him.

"Is there something you need to tell me, Roxxy?" Earl's eyebrow rose high.

"Should there be?"

"I'm just curious as to when you would have time to question Officer Burton." He slid his hands into his pants pocket.

This was a tactic he'd used on her when she was younger. He tried to look curious, and when she was a child, she fell for it every time. Now that she was grown, it wasn't going to work.

"I told you I had time at the tryouts. In between their drills and for a few minutes afterwards when he escorted me to my car."

Earl stared at her. His blue eyes bored into her, and she had to fight the urge to squirm. He had always been the ultra-protective militant father. Tough. Caring. Strict.

But he had one weakness.

His daughter's wide eyes and smile.

"Did I do something wrong?" She turned on the charm and tilted her head to the side.

He'd never been able to resist her innocent act.

Even when she was a child and he had all the evidence that she'd done wrong, one pitiful look from Roxxy would break him.

"No, you didn't." He chuckled.

She relaxed a little and smiled. It had worked like a charm. She knew her father well.

"Yesterday when I went down to the hotel lobby to snag a cup of coffee, I just happened to see Officer Burton coming from the elevators and leaving. You wouldn't know anything about that now, would you?"

Roxxy froze, her smile still in place.

Shit.

She maintained eye contact with him for she knew if she cut away, it would be a dead giveaway she was not telling the truth.

Instead, she shrugged and tried to act nonchalant. "I wouldn't know. This is a small city after all."

"Is that so?" he murmured.

She stood on her tiptoes and laid a kiss on his cheek. "Love you, Daddy. See you in a little bit."

Roxxy escaped from the room and breathed a sigh of relief. Her feet carried her as fast as they could in heels without running to put some distance between her and her father.

She didn't want to give him the chance to call her back into the room.

Nope.

Not going to even have that conversation with him.

Exciting the precinct, she caught sight of Phil pulling up to the door. She hopped in the car. "Let's roll."

"We should have gone in immediately from the moment we knew he had barricaded himself in the fucking building," Myles growled. He leaned a hand against the BEAR. Pissed off didn't even describe what he was feeling.

Those two women hadn't deserved to die in the manner they had. According to the sisters of the suspect, Adrienne, the ex-girlfriend, had broken up with Darius six months ago—he had not taken the breakup well.

"They were dead before we even got here," Ash replied, keeping his voice low.

Myles wanted to tear into something.

SWAT was to protect the people of the city against bad men like Darius Sherman.

Innocent until proven guilty.

Myles released a snort.

How much proving did they need to do?

The man had been outside popping off a few shots and then went inside. The poor women had been shot up by the power of a semiautomatic weapon that had been confiscated from the scene.

"No one heard anything? No one called the cops?" Myles blew out a frustrated breath.

This was the downside to the job.

Not being able to rescue the innocent.

"There's no telling. Not that it's an excuse, but the people of the neighborhood hear gunshots every day. Who knows what they were thinking." Ash laid a hand on Myles's shoulder.

Zain and Iker came to stand next to them. Their faces revealed they felt the same as Myles.

"Offer still stands tonight. Drinks on me," Iker announced somberly. He took his helmet off and ran his hand through his short hair. "This shit is fucked up. A person can't even go to bed without a crazed maniac running in and shooting up the fucking place."

Silence filled the air. Myles glanced over at the house. A chill snaked its way down Myles's spine. It never got any better. No matter how many times he'd seen a dead body at the scene of a crime, it didn't make it any easier.

Death wasn't something one could become numb to.

Not Myles.

His entire life, he'd been trained to protect and serve.

"Looks like we have company." Zain tipped his head toward something behind them.

They glanced in the direction where he was staring.

A silver sedan pulled up and parked next to a few patrol cars. Myles knew before he saw her that it was Roxxy.

He greedily took her form in once she stepped from the car. Her feet were encased in heels, and she had on a business suit with a skirt that stopped appropriately at her knees.

But it didn't matter.

Myles knew what those thighs looked like straddling his face.

An older man about late forties exited the driver's side and walked around to her side. She smiled at him, and Myles instantly didn't care for the man.

She should only smile at him like that.

"Shit, the auditors are here." Declan came to stand next to Myles.

"What's the word from the medical examiner?" Myles tore his gaze away from Roxxy.

Mac joined them. His infamous scowl was in place. "Doc said from the dried blood and the bodies' temperatures, that it would appear the women have been dead at least twenty-four to thirty-six hours."

Curses went around.

"So that fucker has been going in and out the house while they lay dying?" Brodie exclaimed.

"That will tell you how sick he is." Zain shook his head.

"Heads up," Iker murmured.

"Hello, gentlemen," a familiar southern accent sounded behind him.

Myles turned and found Roxxy standing with the other auditor. Myles had met him once, and his name evaded him.

Not that he wanted to remember the man who he wanted to punch in the face.

"Ms. Sutton." Mac stepped forward and took her hand in a shake. "This isn't really a good time right now."

"Oh?" She held a binder to her chest and glanced around at the scene.

Myles knew when her gaze landed on the medical examiner's vans. Her body stiffened, and the smile faded from her face.

"I see. No one from the team—"

"We're all here and fine," Myles interrupted her.

She spun to face him, and Myles had to fight stepping toward her. The gentle breeze that blew slid her hair across her eyes. She lifted her hand and tucked the offending strands behind her ear.

"Well, be that as it may, we still have a job to do.

This gives us another scenario to write up." She glanced over at her partner. "I believe you all have met, Phil."

Greetings went around. The men shifted their stances. Myles detected that none of them wanted to go through this.

Not even Mac or Declan.

"This may seem like an odd time, but there are some questions we just need to ask. Nothing that will impede on the reports that will be due to your captain," Phil assured them.

"I just need to speak to who was in charge." Roxxy turned toward Mac and Declan.

"I took control." Mac raised a hand.

"Was there a need for a negotiator?" Phil asked.

Ash raised his hand. Phil waved for him to follow him. Ash blew out a deep breath and left with the auditor.

"I'll just need a few minutes of your time, Sergeant," Roxxy noted.

"Sure." Mac faced the rest of them. "Pack up and prepare to go back to the precinct."

He guided Roxxy away, and Myles couldn't help but watch the sway of her hips as she walked off with Mac.

"Someone's infatuated with the auditor chick." Zain slapped Myles on the back of his shoulder.

"Fuck off," Myles growled. He followed him to the open compartments on the BEAR. He lifted the shield and placed it inside.

"She's a fox. You'd be crazy not to be." Iker snorted.

"When you find a good woman—" Declan was cut off by their groans.

"Oh, puh-lease, spare us," Brodie begged.

They all laughed at Declan's expense. He held up his hand with his middle finger extended.

"Let's do as we were ordered," Myles said. He tried to steer the conversation away from Roxxy. There was no way he'd be spilling the beans on what went on between the two of them. Some things a man kept to himself. "Plus, I'm feeling the need to have quite a few drinks on your tab."

12

Roxxy walked out of her bedroom and pulled the ties of her silk robe tighter. It had been an extremely long day. With the two casualties on the SWAT call today, it left her with additional reports that needed to be filled.

Tomorrow was the last day of auditing, and that would mean once she returned home, she'd finish up her findings and submit them to her father. After Earl reviewed them, if nothing else was needed, then everything would be forwarded to the captain and mayor.

The television was on, but the volume was low. The news was on, and the top story was that of the hostage situation. Roxxy ignored it and went over to the desk where her computer was waiting for her.

"Roxxy's all work and no play," she murmured, sitting in the chair. She opened her computer and opened the last report she had been working on before she'd gone and taken a shower. Her hair was tucked up in a bun on top of her head. The warm water had help relax her muscles.

At the scene earlier that day, she'd caught sight of Myles, and she had wanted to run to him. After learning that the SWAT team had apprehended the suspect, but hostages had already been deceased, it broke her heart. The men all were affected by it. She could even see it when she'd spoken with Mac. He'd appeared gruffer and more irritated. She hadn't taken much of his time. What she would need for her reports would be in his.

Seeing Myles in all of his gear and sweaty would be ingrained in her head forever. She wanted to go to him and hug him. Comfort him. Losing victims was never easy. She'd been witness to other teams who had been too late and lost the very people they were trying to save. It was the gruesome reality that most people didn't see. The news always focused on the victims and families, but no one ever thought about the first responders who were the ones who made the discoveries or were the ones trying to save them.

They were always forgotten.

Roxxy wished Myles was here. She'd ensure he would be taken care of.

If only for one more night.

By noon tomorrow, they'd be on the road headed back to Klinedale. It was a small town that boasted a community of about five thousand people. Almost everyone knew everyone.

This time tomorrow, she would be tucked away in her own bed, away from Columbia. Away from Myles.

Once she was gone, would he even think of her?

He'd given her much to fantasize about.

She sniffed and tried to compose herself. Typing a few commands out on the keyboard, she froze at the sound of a knock at the door.

"Who the hell is that?" She glanced at the time stamp on her computer and found it a little after eleven at night. This wouldn't be her father. He would be fast asleep at this time of night.

She stood and opened the drawer to the desk and pulled out her small gun. Her other weapons were in the bedroom.

This one would do.

She crossed the room without a sound, comforted by the steel in her hand.

Stopping in front of the door, she rose and looked through the peephole and froze.

She left the chain on the door, turned the bottom lock, and opened it slightly. "Myles?"

"Hey, Roxxy."

She swallowed hard. He was dressed in a dark shirt with CPD on it with jeans and boots. He leaned against the wall.

"Hey, yourself." She tightened her grip on the gun, unable to believe he was there.

In the flesh.

"Are you going to let me in or are you going to leave me out here?"

His deep baritone caressed her, sending a tingle down to her core. Her breasts grew heavy while her nipples turned into hard buds. The silky material slid across them, and she almost moaned out loud. His gaze dropped down to her chest, and his nostrils flared.

He knew the effect he had on her.

"Please. Come in." She heard the huskiness of her voice and frankly didn't care. There was no question why he was showing up at her hotel. She pushed the door shut and took the chain off. She opened it and stepped back into the room.

He entered, and with his size, the room suddenly appeared smaller. The door shut behind him, and he replaced the chain.

She swallowed hard.

He turned back to her and tipped his head to the weapon in her hand.

"Are you planning on using that tonight?" His lips curled up in the corner.

She glanced down at the pink gun and shook her head. "Not unless you give me a reason."

"Why don't we put that up then, because I promise, you won't have a reason to shoot me." He moved to her and gently reached down and took the gun from her. "Where you want it?"

The scent of his cologne captivated her. Her pussy clenched with need.

It had to be a sin to smell that good.

"The desk." She stood frozen in place watching him walk over and put it back in the drawer. "Myles."

He stalked back to her, his intense gaze locked on her. He reached for her and crushed her to him. Her breath escaped her as his mouth covered hers.

There was no need to speak.

It was like he'd known she needed him.

What the hell would she do once she returned home?

His tongue plundered her mouth, instantly taking control of the kiss. She tasted the slight hint of alcohol and mint.

Roxxy leaned into him, allowing him the control.

She gripped the bottom of his shirt and pulled it over his head, breaking them apart. She tossed it over her shoulder. Her hands went to his belt.

His went to her robe.

He parted the silk material and released a curse.

"You are perfection," he murmured.

"As are you," she breathed, leaning her face against his chest. She successfully opened his belt and went for the button of his pants. A shiver slid down her spine as the soft material fell down. She released him to allow it to fall to the floor, leaving her completely naked. Her core ached to have him between her legs.

He kicked off his shoes. She helped him push down his pants. She knelt on the floor in front of him. Her reward sprang free once they removed his final piece of clothing.

Without waiting, she reached for his long, thick cock and brought it to her lips. She licked the entire length of it before coming back to the wide, blunt tip.

"Yes," he hissed.

She met his gaze and held it while she wrapped her lips around the tip of his dick. She slowly introduced it into her mouth. He threaded his fingers in her hair, displacing the bun from the top of her head.

Moisture collected at the apex of her thighs.

She had been craving the feeling of Myles's hard body underneath her fingertips.

Roxxy took her time worshipping the man before her.

His dick was one that should be cherished.

Using both of her hands, she gripped him and ran them up and down his shaft in tandem with her mouth. She hummed and took great pleasure in wringing every moan and gasp from Myles.

His hold tightened in her hair.

She could feel a tremble snaking its way through him.

She had him.

She opened her eyes and looked up. He stood there, his muscles tensed with his brow slightly furrowed. His chest was rising and falling fast.

This big strong man is putty in my hands.

Roxxy wanted to see him fall apart.

Never had she ever wanted to please someone before.

She increased her pace and hold on his shaft.

"Roxxy," he called out.

She ignored the slight pain from her hair being pulled and relished the fact that she was sending him over the brink of orgasm. His hips thrust forward. She allowed him to fuck her mouth. The slight taste of saltiness met her tongue, and she knew he was close. She held on to him tight and sucked harder, refusing to take her eyes off him.

His eyes flew open and met hers. With a shout, he paused his hips while his salty release flowed into her mouth.

Roxxy swallowed every drop.

His breaths were coming fast as if he'd just run a marathon.

Roxxy's heart swelled.

"Come here," he growled, pulling his cock from her

mouth. He reached down and yanked her up into a standing position. He swung her up and tossed her over his shoulder.

"Myles!" She laughed.

"I've warned you about that mouth of yours." He swatted her bottom.

She gasped from the sting of it, and if she didn't know any better, she liked it.

He carried her into the bedroom and deposited her on the middle of the bed.

He didn't give her time to move. He braced himself over her. His intense eyes bored into hers. She reached up and cupped his bearded face, memorizing every detail.

Myles leaned down and brushed his lips against hers. It sent a rush of energy through her body. He blazed a trail down her skin.

She immediately opened her legs for him, knowing where his end goal was.

The second his lips closed around her clit, her body arched off the mattress.

"Myles," she cried out. Her hands flew over her head, and she gripped the blanket tight.

There was no mistaking that Myles had just claimed her pussy. He might as well tattoo his name on her. His tongue slid between her folds, teasing her.

Her body was his playground.

He worked her up into a fever. Sweat lined her body as she writhed.

Myles used his strong forearms to keep her legs open for him.

God Almighty.

Her hips moved on their own accord, her clit riding his tongue.

He introduced not one, but two fingers deep inside her.

"Ah...shit," she gasped. She tried to scoot away, but his arm clamped down on her.

"Where do you think you're going?" His low growl sent goosebumps along her skin.

She brushed her hair from her face and met his intense stare. "It's too much...I can't—"

"Who's stopping you, Roxxy?"

He gave her pussy one long lick, and her eyes rolled back. She fell back against the bed and gave up the fight.

He could do whatever he wanted.

Roxxy floated among the clouds. Myles fucked her with his fingers while he teased her clit. He tugged on her swollen bundle of nerves, and her body tightened.

A scream erupted from her lips.

Her orgasm slammed into her like a freight train.

Her muscles tensed, and she reached for anything

to hold on to for fear her body would float away amongst the waves of her release.

She dug her nails into Myles's strong shoulders.

Her arms fell to the sides as he climbed over her. He braced himself over her. She opened her eyes and met his cocky smile.

How could she walk away from this man?

"What are we doing?" she asked quietly, finally able to catch her breath. She reached up and trailed a finger across his lips. They were still wet from her, and her core clenched.

"If you have to ask, then I'm not doing it right." His eyes crinkled in the corners with his smile.

"I'm serious. I told you I've never had a one-night stand before, and now you're back..."

She blinked. She wasn't made for this. She could feel herself growing attached to Myles. They'd only know each other a few days, and already she dreaded the long ride home.

"I couldn't get you out of my head," he admitted, turning serious. He brushed her cheek with her finger and stared at her with wonder in his eyes.

"What does that mean?" she whispered.

He settled into the valley of her thighs. His hard cock teased her opening, and she bit back a groan.

"Maybe I don't want just one night." His lips

pressed against hers in a soft kiss. He pulled back and placed another one on her chin.

She turned her head to allow him to reach the hollow of her neck. Her breasts were crushed between them.

"But I don't live here in Columbia."

"Not sure if you know this." His lips skimmed her skin and sent an electric current through her body. "But there was an invention that allows you to get in and go to whatever destination you want. You can travel quite a distance in it, too."

She giggled. "Is that so?"

"Yeah, they call them cars."

He licked and nipped her skin until he came back to her lips. He captured her mouth in the sweetest of kisses that completely took her breath away. She could still taste the tanginess of herself. She returned the kiss with the same fervor.

"I think I've heard of 'em." She laid her country twang on stronger, and his dick jerked against her leg.

Hmm...someone liked her drawl.

"Good. Now when do you leave?"

"Tomorrow after our final sign-out with your captain."

"Is that so?"

Myles pushed off the bed and flipped her over onto her stomach. He hefted her up onto her knees. She spread her legs wide, anticipating what was to come. The blunt tip of his cock nestled itself between her slick folds.

"Well, looks like we are going to have to make the most of the time we have left."

He sank deep into her, and they both released a groan.

She balled her hands into tight fists, bunching the sheets in them.

Myles pulled back and slammed hard inside her, eliciting a cry to spill from her lips.

She prayed morning didn't come too fast.

13

"If you check your phone one more time, I'm going to take it and throw it out that window over there," Ash murmured.

Myles lifted his head and glanced at his friend. They were seated in the conference room waiting for Mac and Declan to enter. Leaving Roxxy's hotel this morning had been one of the hardest things he had ever done.

Her mussed hair, swollen lips, and perfect skin had him wanting to stay, but they both had to get to work.

"I'm not doing anything but browsing the internet," he replied.

"Sure you are. I know that look." Ash chuckled. He leaned back in his chair with an all-knowing glint in his eyes.

Here we go.

"We all know that look," Iker chimed in from behind him.

"Shut up." Myles tried to ignore their heckling.

"Where'd you go when you left the bar last night?" Zain asked.

"None of your fucking business, that's where." He turned around and found all eyes on him.

The entire team had gone out to their favorite pub and had a few rounds of drinks. Whenever they had a hard call, they blew off steam. By the third rounds of drinks, he couldn't get Roxxy out of his mind. He didn't have her number to call or text her so he did the next best thing.

Showed up at her hotel room late at night.

He had been half expecting her to close the door in his face, but instead she had opened the it, standing in nothing but a silk robe holding a pink Glock.

Now that's a woman.

There was no way in hell he was telling them anything about what went on between him and Roxxy. Before Roxxy, he'd share a story or two with women he'd been with.

But not this time.

Not Roxxy.

His lips were sealed.

"I think I know where he went," Iker teased.

"Oh, I know my friend quite well. I'm sure I can guess, too." Ash barked a laugh. "It had something to do with a little sexy auditor."

Myles raised both hands in the air with his middle fingers extended.

"Myles not sharing details means only one thing," Brodie announced.

"He's pussy-whipped," Iker and Zain shouted simultaneously.

"A pussy has tamed the all mighty Myles Burton." Brodie cackled.

Myles snickered and shook his head. He couldn't help it. His teammates were nutcases, and there was no one else he'd rather be on a team with. He turned around in his seat at the sound of the door opening.

"Glad you men are in better sprits," Mac said, entering the room.

Declan followed close behind and stood next to him. This was a standard meeting SWAT had to discuss important business.

The room simmered down. By the looks of Mac and Declan, they were getting straight to business.

"There's a few things on the agenda we need to go over." Mac paused and placed his hands behind his back. His legendary scowl was on his face.

The room quieted, waiting for him to continue.

"We've gone back over all the notes and details about our potential candidate to join our team. We have extended the offer for an interview to Officer Knight who has accepted. We will be hosting a team interview with her first. Then she'll meet with Dec and myself. We'll regroup afterwards and vote. If she has majority of the vote, then she'll interview with the captain."

"Here's her CV. Take your time and review it. This will give you a background on her and her work history." Declan walked around and handed out the papers to each member of the team. "Make sure you have some good questions for her."

Declan took a seat in the front of the room once he was done.

Knight seemed like a solid candidate. Team interviews gave the men a chance to speak with the prospective member to get to know them, get a feel for them and see if they would blend in. Tryouts were to get a taste of their skills.

Fitting in with the team was everything.

Every man had to be sure they could trust each team member to cover their six.

The meeting continued, with Mac announcing they would be interviewing Knight on Monday morning. Mac spoke about training and upcoming vacations.

Myles reached for his phone. Now that he and Roxxy had officially exchanged numbers, she had promised she'd text him when she was about to leave the precinct. He wanted to at least see her one last time before she got on the road to go home.

Never would he have thought he would consider a relationship with a woman, let alone one who lived a little way away.

Glancing at the screen, he saw he had not missed any messages.

The sound of a whip being cracked filled the air.

Myles's head flew up.

Ash had his face covered, his shoulders shaking.

Myles looked around and found Brodie, Iker, and Zain dying of laughter.

Ash pulled his hand away to reveal tears streaming down his cheeks.

"Ha, ha," Myles snapped. He dropped his phone down on the table and glared at all of them before rotating back to Mac.

"I'm sure someone will catch us up to whatever is going on," Declan said with a small smile on his lips.

"There's nothing for you to be caught—" Myles was cut off by the shrill ringing and buzzing of cell phones. His gaze dropped down to his phone, and he saw it was the dispatcher.

They were getting called out on an assignment.

"SWAT, let's roll out in five minutes," Mac barked.

The sounds of chairs scraping filled the air.

Laughter and jokes were gone.

It was time to suit up.

"Roxxy Lynn, are you going to tell me why you have returned from the city with a glow?"

Roxxy jumped and spun around. Her mother stood behind her with her hip leaning against the counter.

Roxxy bit back a smile. She turned back to the dishes in the sink and washed a plate. There was no way she'd be able to look Shelby Sutton in the eye and tell her a lie.

Her mother could always tell.

"I don't know what you are talking about." She'd been back in town for a few days and had already spoken to Myles a few times. They'd missed each other when she'd submitted all final reports at the station. Apparently, he and the team had been called out on an operation.

"Oh, I think you do." Shelby came to stand beside Roxxy with a drying cloth in her hand. She picked up a dish and wiped it dry before placing it in the cabinet. She bumped Roxxy with her hip playfully. "Go ahead, you can tell me."

A grin spread across her lips. Shelby Sutton had missed her calling in life. She could have been an FBI agent or CIA with the way she sniffed out information.

"Mom, I'm a grown woman."

"Oh, is that how it is?"

The twinkle in Shelby's eyes made Roxxy bite her lip to keep from groaning. They were as close as mother and daughter could be. Growing up, Roxxy had always shared everything with her. From her first crush, her first kiss, to even the crap Korey had pulled on her.

"You've never returned home from an assignment with such a pep in your step."

Did she want to tell her about Myles yet?

That would mean spilling the beans that she'd had a one-night stand with him—twice.

What would she think?

"Okay, okay, okay." Roxxy faced her. She would only tell her the PG version of the story just to get her off her back. "You have to promise not to say a word to Dad."

"I knew it!" Shelby jumped in place with a large smile on her face.

Roxxy rolled her eyes. Looking at her mom was like peering into a mirror that revealed what she'd look like in thirty years.

"I can keep a secret from your father."

"Calm down, geesh." Roxxy snagged a kitchen towel and dried her hands. "If you must know, I met someone."

"A man. I knew it." Her mother paused, her brown eyes growing wide. "Was he handsome?"

"Yes," Roxxy sighed, thinking of Myles's devilish good looks. She couldn't fight the silly grin from spreading now. Just thinking of Myles had her feeling all giddy inside. "He's tall, muscular, bald head."

"I'm liking what I'm hearing so far."

"Mom!" Roxxy burst out laughing at her mom's response.

"I may be your mother, but I'm still a woman." Shelby shrugged.

Jesus, help me. Roxxy closed her eyes, not wanting to go down the train of thought of Shelby being a 'woman'.

"Too much information," she muttered, turning back to the sink. She dove her hands in the warm soapy water in search of the next plate. After she'd finished cleaning the dishes she would take Sunshine for a run. Whenever she was gone too many days in a row, her faithful mare knew. Roxxy would have to go groveling for forgiveness. A nice bag of apples always seemed to do the trick. Sunshine would be eating out of her hands in no time and all would be forgiven.

"Hush, girl. Now finish telling me about Mr. Tall and Muscular. What's his name?"

"Myles Burton. He's on the SWAT team. Former Army—"

"Any good in bed?"

"Mom!" she exclaimed. She faced Shelby in shock.

If she had pearls around her neck, she'd be clutching them now. She stood unable to form any words.

"Now don't go looking at me like that. You got here somehow, and it was not immaculate conception." Her mother pushed Roxxy out of the way. She gripped the dishrag from the water and wrung it. She let the water out and hummed like it was any other day they'd cleaned the kitchen together.

"For all I care to know I was delivered by a big white stork." Roxxy threw her hands up in the air and stepped away from her. There was no way she was thinking of her parents having sexual relations to conceive her.

The stork came, dropped off baby Roxxy Lynn, and that was how it had gone down.

"You still haven't answered my question, but I already got my answer. It's written all over your face." Shelby wiped down the countertops and shook her hand in the air at Roxxy.

"I'm done with this conversation." Roxxy chuckled. She moved back to the sink and ran the water to rinse out the final suds. They had cleaned the kitchen countless amounts of times tougher, and working beside her mother was second nature.

"I just hope he treats you better than Korey," Shelby muttered.

Roxxy paused at what she was doing. When it

came to Korey and Myles, there was no comparing them. Myles didn't have a dishonest bone in his body. Korey, on the other hand, she didn't trust him as far as she could throw him. She glanced out the window and stared off onto the lands that surrounded the house. The Sutton farm was full of lush greenery. It was where she'd grown up and it would always be a part of her. "In the small amount of time I've known him, he's practically wiped Korey from my memory."

"Sounds like he's a good man then," Shelby replied quietly.

Roxxy turned and met her mom's wise gaze. "He is."

"I can't wait to meet him."

Roxxy shut off the water and glanced around the kitchen. She hadn't realized how much time had passed. The kitchen practically glowed. Now she would go for a ride. She couldn't wait. The feel of having her horse beneath her and the wind blowing through her hair was one of her favorite outdoor activities.

"We're going to take it a day at a time. You know, test the waters out."

"That's smart."

"Yeah. I just don't want to be hurt again the way Korey did me." She grew silent thinking of all the hateful things Korey had said to her. As if she'd driven him to cheat on her. He hadn't been a man and taken responsibility for his actions—no, according to him, it was her fault.

"Listen, baby." She took Roxxy by her hands and entwined their fingers together.

Roxxy stared up at her and felt as if she were a teenager again. Shelby had a knack for calming Roxxy down.

"The man upstairs didn't mean for you to end up with Korey. That was divine intervention to show you the type of man Korey truly is."

Roxxy blinked back the tears that threatened to fall. Leave it up to her mother to go deep.

"He didn't have to make it hurt so bad," she whispered. She could have thought of about ten different ways God could have told her that Korey wasn't the one.

"How would you learn? If it would have been an easy breakup, then you wouldn't have appreciated the valuable lesson. You know I always say there is something to be learned from each situation we find ourselves in."

"Ain't that the truth," Roxxy mumbled.

Korey had taught her a very hard lesson.

One she hoped to never repeat again.

14

Myles walked out of the locker room sore, pissed, and tired. That combination did not go well together. He was on a short fuse. In the last three days, SWAT had gone out on four missions. He didn't know what was going on in the city.

There was a reason for this.

He headed toward the exit. He was going to attempt to make it home and get a few hours of shut-eye.

Zain and Iker had chosen to stay and nap in one of the bunker rooms. Ash, Declan, and Mac all had women at home waiting for them. They would be headed out in a minute. Myles couldn't stomach the domestic chatter between the guys and opted to leave now.

What waited for him was his king-size bed and massive pillows. They were currently calling his name.

To go home and have Roxxy lying across his bed, naked and waiting for him...

Shit.

Slow down, man.

Myles wasn't one to have a relationship, so this was foreign territory for him.

Well tonight, he may not have Roxxy waiting in his bed for him, but he'd have the next best thing.

FaceTime.

"Burton!" a voice shouted out behind him.

Myles turned and saw Reeves striding toward him with a furious expression. His partner, Cruz, was right behind him.

"What is it, Reeves?" He adjusted the duffle bag strap on his shoulder.

"I'm going to kick your ass."

Myles let go of his duffle bag, uncaring that it landed on the floor. Reeves had another think coming if he thought he could take on Myles.

"Watch what you say, Reeves. I might take that as a real threat," he growled. Myles grew tense as Reeves approached. He had about a good four inches and around thirty pounds on the man.

"Why didn't I get chosen to move forward? This is my second time trying out. I did everything that was recommended." Reeves stopped in front of Myles.

"Come on, man. Let's go walk it off," Cruz said, grabbing Reeves by the arm.

"Get off me." Reeves snatched his arm back. He turned to Myles with hatred brimming in his eyes. "I want Burton to explain to me the reason I didn't get to move forward."

"Back up off me, Reeves," Myles warned. He really didn't feel like ending up getting his ass chewed out by the captain for knocking Reeves out. The suspension would not be worth it.

"Or what? If you hadn't had had your eyes on the auditor bitch, maybe you would have seen my skills."

"What the fuck did you just say?" Myles stepped forward.

Reeves had crossed the line.

"I mean, she was a nice piece of ass to have around, but you're fucking with my career." Reeves stepped closer. He pressed his pointer finger against Myles's chest.

Myles knocked Reeves's finger off him. He didn't take his eyes off the asshole.

"Don't touch me." His voice dipped low. He could feel his rage rising. No one would speak ill of Roxxy.

No one.

"What the hell is going on over here?" Mac stormed out of the locker room with Declan and Ash right behind him.

"This motherfucker here blew my chance for SWAT." Reeves pointed in Myles's face.

Myles knocked it out of the way and pushed Reeves away from him.

"I blew your chance?" Myles roared, no longer able to control his fury. Reeves should be man enough to take responsibility for his own fuckups. If he didn't make SWAT, it was his own damn fault. "How about you're not fit to wear SWAT on your chest!"

"You son of a bitch!" Reeves swung his fist.

Myles blocked it and shoved Reeves back into Cruz. Arms clamped around him, keeping him from following Cruz.

"He's not worth it," Ash snapped.

"Let it go, big guy. Walk away," Declan ordered. He pulled Myles backward.

"Reeves, leave! Now!" Mac positioned himself between the two of them.

Myles glared at Reeves from around Mac. His muscles were tensed, and his breaths were coming fast.

The son of a bitch was lucky.

Had his teammates not come out of the locker room when they had, Myles's fist would be going upside his face.

"All of you can go fuck yourselves!" Reeves struggled against Cruz.

"Let's go," Cruz said. "You don't want to be a part of their shitty team anyway."

"What the fuck you say, Cruz?" Myles dove after him.

Ash and Declan tightened their hold on him.

"Get him out of here." Mac pointed toward the front of the precinct.

Apparently having heard the commotion, a crowd stood at the end of the hall.

Cruz finally got Reeves to about face and walk away. Reeves continued to shout obscenities until he disappeared from sight.

Myles's hands were balled into fists. It wasn't until he didn't see Reeves anymore that he turned his attention to Mac.

"I'm good." He shook Ash and Declan off of him. He rubbed his face with a trembling hand. He needed to get out of there. He needed to burn off this adrenaline and energy.

"There's nothing to see here." Mac motioned for the curious bystanders to move. Once the last person was gone, he faced Myles. "Let's go outside and get you some fresh air."

Myles reached for his bag that had been kicked out of the way during the scuffle. He followed Mac through the doors he had originally been heading to. They walked into the parking lot toward where his truck was waiting. He opened the driver's door and tossed his bag in.

"What the hell happened back there?" Ash asked. He tunneled his fingers through his hair before folding his arms in front of his chest and focusing on Myles.

"Reeves accused me of blowing his shot on SWAT." Myles tried to remain calm. He took a few deep breaths and willed his heart to stop racing.

"You blew his shot?" Mac's low voice cut through the air. "When did he ever have one?"

"Ya'll already know my thoughts on him," Declan drawled. Yeah, they all did. Declan didn't make no qualms about his feeling for the beat cop. "I wished he would have run up on me."

Myles nodded. Without a doubt, Declan would have whipped his ass. He'd been waiting for a reason to say something to Reeves.

"Why would he just go after you? It was a team decision," Mac said. Always the voice of reason. "If he had a compliant, he could have come to me, or hell, even the captain."

"Don't know, don't care." Myles leaned back on his truck. At the moment, he didn't give a rat's ass. "But I will tell you one thing. If he runs up on me again, just move the fuck out of the way."

"As much as I would love to see you beat the piss

out of him, we can't have blue fighting blue," Mac statcd.

Myles released a curse at Mac trying to be reasonable.

"He's right. We're up against enough as it is, we don't need cop versus cop," Declan chimed in.

"Well then, you go tell that to him!" Myles growled, pointing at the building. He pushed off the vehicle, anger still brimming in his chest.

Ash shifted his position and stood before Myles.

"Leave." Ash motioned to the truck. "Go home. Go for a run or something to blow off steam."

Myles blew out a frustrated breath and threw his hands up.

"Fine. I'm out of here."

He grabbed the handle and swung open the door and got in his truck. He ignored Mac calling his name and hit the start button. The truck roared to life. He threw the car in drive and pulled out of his spot. He turned onto the street and hit the gas.

Roxxy rushed over to her nightstand. The sound of her phone ringing cut through the air.

She had a date tonight.

A virtual date.

With Myles.

She snatched her phone up and slid her finger across the screen. Fresh from the shower, she wanted to look her best after a day of riding. She didn't want to appear as if she'd been out on the farm all day.

Myles's face came on the screen, and Roxxy's heart raced.

"Hey there, handsome," she greeted him with a wide smile. She climbed into her bed and propped herself up on the headboard.

"Hey, Roxxy girl. How are you?" Myles's deep voice met her ears. He looked dead on his feet and agitated.

Alarms went off.

Something was wrong.

"I'm good now you're on the phone with me." She offered a smile to try to get one from him. His lips curved up slightly, but it wasn't the same. "What's wrong?"

He smoothed a hand over his cheek and shook his head. "Nothing. I don't want to burden you with work-related shit."

She relaxed against the pillows. She had been worried for nothing. She understood his job was full of stress, and tension was expected for a SWAT officer.

She could help relieve his stress. She'd help take his mind off what was bothering him.

"Ah, honey, I'm sorry work sucked." She pouted a little, allowing her spaghetti strap of her nightgown to fall to the side.

His quick intake of breath could be heard. She bit back a laugh.

Got him.

"Why don't you tell me about it?" She was laying her accent on strong. She flung her hair over her shoulder and focused her attention on Myles. She'd been waiting for this call all day.

His eyes darkened, and he brought the phone closer. He fussed with the pillow behind his head before he seemed comfortable lying across his bed. "Not much to tell. Reeves blamed me for him not making SWAT—"

"How was that your fault?" she asked. Roxxy remembered Reeves. He was cocky and confident he was going to make the team. In the short time she'd been around the men, she could see that he wouldn't have fit in. He had been trying too hard.

"Hell if I know. He almost caught a beatdown." Myles gave a dry chuckle.

"Oh, really?" Her eyebrow jumped up in surprise. "You would have beat him up?"

"Fuck yeah. The punk would have deserved it, too." Myles's lips curved up into a grin.

There he is.

167

"You're much bigger than him. It wouldn't have been a fair fight." She giggled, thinking of Myles's size. A shiver ran through her at the memory of him pressed against her.

"Well, he came at me like a big man, he would have been treated as one." Myles lifted his shoulders. "Enough about me. How was your day?"

Roxxy bit her lip and ran a finger over her chest. "It was okay. Relaxed today and did some things around the farm for my parents. I'll be going into the office tomorrow."

She had taken the day to do chores. It wasn't anything glamorous to share. She had been downright dirty before she'd jumped in the shower. She didn't want to take this call looking like she'd mucked stalls.

She didn't know why, but she missed Myles. In the short time they'd spent together, he'd grown on her.

"Where's your next assignment?" Myles's voice grew deeper.

She slipped her finger to the other tiny shoulder strap and slid it off her. "Not sure yet."

"What are you doing, Roxxy?"

Roxxy widened her eyes, appearing innocent. She shrugged nonchalantly. "Getting more comfortable. Is that okay with you?"

"Yeah." Myles released a cough. He cleared his throat. "Whatever makes you happy."

She smiled at him, allowing the nightie to completely fall away from her, baring her naked breasts. Tonight she may not be with Myles, but they could have a little fun. She felt adventurous with him staring at her.

"I'm happy." She propped her hand under her mounds and ensured Myles got the full view of them. "Are you happy?"

"Fuck no." He grunted.

"Why not?" she asked innocently. She skimmed her fingers over her smooth skin and arrived at her beaded nipple. She pinched it, allowing a slight moan to escape from her lips.

"Because those pretty nipples belong in my mouth."

Roxxy's core clenched with need. Just imagining Myles's lips closing around her bud had her groaning.

Maybe this wasn't such a good idea after all.

She'd never been involved with someone long distance before. This was new territory for her.

"Really?" she whispered. She didn't have a snarky comeback.

"Yeah, really. Do me a favor, Roxxy girl." Myles paused.

"What is it?" She cupped her breast and gently massaged it.

"Take the nightgown off and let me see all of you."

She grinned and stood from the bed. Holding the phone away from her, she allowed the gown to shimmy down her body and fall to the floor.

"Jesus, you're beautiful," Myles breathed.

Roxxy ran her hand down her side and rested it on her hip. She knew she had curves and was thick in the right places. She wasn't ashamed of it either.

"Why am I the only one naked?" She pouted.

"Seriously?" Myles barked a laugh.

Roxxy sat back on her bed and angled the phone to where it only showed her face.

"Um, if you get to see all of me, it's only fair that you take it all off, too!" She paused. "If not, then my clothes are going to go back on."

"I got you."

He put the phone down, and the only thing she could see was the ceiling.

"Take it off! Take it off," she chanted playfully.

Within a few seconds, Myles came back into view on his phone. His bare chest was visible. Her fingers itched to run through the tiny sprinkle of hair that was on display.

"There. Satisfied?" His eyebrow rose high.

"Oh, no, Officer Burton. I want to see it all." She wagged her eyebrows.

He stared at her. Even through the phone, his intense stare gave her butterflies.

She bit her lip and waited.

"Damn it, Roxxy. I want you here with me."

"Stop stalling, Burton. Show me the goods," she demanded.

He muttered something incomprehensible. The screen shifted, and before Roxxy knew it, Myles had his dick on display for her. It was fully engorged, and he was slowly rubbing the shaft with his hand.

Oh, this wasn't a good idea at all.

Her core clenched, and she was mesmerized by the sight.

They were past the point of no return.

"Lie back on your bed, Roxxy."

Myles's voice broke through her naughty thoughts. She needed this more than she needed to breathe.

Her heart rate was racing, and all she could think about was having Myles push his thick cock inside her.

Memories of the taste of it came to mind. She licked her lips, wishing he was here with her.

She did as she was told and rested back on her pillows.

"Myles," she whispered, moisture collecting at the apex of her thighs. She was soaked and ready for him.

Too bad Myles was miles away.

"Not now, Roxxy. We're about to make the most of tonight."

15

Roxxy browsed through rack of negligees, and her cheeks heated. She couldn't even remember a time where she was excited about a sexy piece of silk and lace that she'd wear for a brief moment before it hit the floor.

It had been a few days since her virtual date with Myles.

Her breath caught in her throat at the memory of her pleasuring herself while he gave her commands over the phone.

Roxxy felt young and free.

Their virtual date had grown explosive with the both of them helping the other reach their climax.

Soon they would need to see each other. If ever there was a time she regretted living with her parents, it was now.

It wasn't like she could invite Myles to come stay with her. She doubted her parents would go for that.

Her hand brushed a navy-blue lace teddy, and she paused.

She pulled it from the rack and held it up. It was downright sexy and would barely cover all of her private areas.

"Can I help you?" A woman came to stand beside her.

"I'm just looking around," she automatically replied.

"I'm Karen. Just to let you know, we're running a thirty percent off sale on the entire store." Karen gave her a warm smile.

Of course it would be on sale.

Her gaze wandered back to it. The soft lace in her hand was tempting.

"Why don't you try it on?" Karen asked, apparently recognizing the mental debate going on in Roxxy's brain.

Oh, Karen is good.

"Okay." Roxxy nodded. She followed behind Karen toward the dressing room. She didn't even know how she ended up in the lingerie store. She had stopped at the plaza to run to the post office as a favor for her mother. She'd walked past the lingerie store and suddenly found herself inside browsing.

They entered a small room at the back that had a few discreet rooms for patrons.

"Let me know if there is anything else you need." Karen waved to an empty room.

"Thanks." Roxxy shut the door behind her and faced the mirror inside the private area. She held the pretty garment up to herself and smiled.

She tossed her purse down on the chair in the corner and stripped her clothes off. The cool lace material was heavenly against her naked skin.

Roxxy fixed her hair and stared at her reflection.

There was a sexy diva staring back at her that she didn't recognize.

Hot damn.

She was one sexy bitch.

She posed and found herself laughing out loud at her antics.

It wasn't often that she went shopping for negligees, and especially not something as revealing and sensual as this. The navy-blue color made her skin tone appear even warmer and flawless. The lace between her breasts dipped down low, barely leaving anything to the imagination, and the bottom of it brushed her mid-thigh.

If she bent over, she would be completely exposed.

Myles would love to pull it off her.

She giggled at the thought.

Hell, thinking about it had her heating up.

Grabbing her phone, she took a few quick pictures of herself in the mirror.

She sent one picture to Myles in a text.

Hope you are having a wonderful day, she typed out.

She didn't know who this new Roxxy was, but she was loving the freedom.

She jumped at a knock on her door.

"Everything okay in there?" Karen asked.

"Yes, I love it." Roxxy spun around one last time and glanced at herself over her shoulder.

Karen gave a short laugh. "I knew you would. I recognized the look on your face."

"Yes, and it's in my favorite color, too." Roxxy sighed. She tossed her phone back in her purse and carefully removed the teddy.

"I can go take it up to the register and get it ready for you," Karen offered.

"Thanks." Roxxy snagged her shirt and held it up to herself so she could crack open the door slightly. She handed the negligees to Karen.

"Anything else I can help you find?"

"I think that will be all," Roxxy chuckled. She shut the door and quickly put her clothes back on.

Ideas floated around in her head. She had to find some way where she could either go visit Myles or get him to come down to see her.

Last night's virtual date was amazing, but it wasn't the real thing. Nothing could replace the feel of a real man. Roxxy wanted to be wrapped up in Myles's arms —she needed the have him inside her.

He was growing on her. She didn't know what or how to classify them, but she just knew they were taking it one day at a time.

She exited the dressing room and went to pay for her purchase. She left the store with a wide grin.

She strolled down the sidewalk back toward her car. Her phone vibrated in her purse. She dug it out and saw a text from Myles.

This just made my day. That would look great on my bedroom floor.

Roxxy bit her lip. Should she be forward and ask when they could see each other?

"Oh, what the hell," she mumbled.

When can I see you again?

Afraid to see his response, she threw her phone back in her purse and continued to her car.

"Roxxy!" a familiar voice called out.

Her stomach instantly churned. She'd know that country twang anywhere.

She stopped in her tracks and groaned. She looked behind her and had to fight to keep the scowl from forming.

Korey.

A wide smile was plastered on his face as he sauntered toward her. The urge to run grew in her chest. She had never wanted to see him again, but in their small town, that would be hard.

"How are you, baby?" he asked.

"You don't get to call me that," she answered haughtily. She shifted her purse up on her shoulder and glared at him.

"Don't be like that. We need to talk." He came to stand in front of her.

She automatically took a step backward. He apparently chose to ignore her hard stare.

"There's nothing we need to say to each other."

"What you have there in the bag?" His gaze dropped down to her hands.

She tightened her grip on the handle. "None of your business." She sniffed.

He moved closer to her and reached to lay a hand on her shoulder. She retreated away from him, refusing to allow him to touch her.

"I don't recall you shopping there before."

"I never had a reason until now." She rolled her eyes and glanced down at her watch. Maybe he would get the hint.

"What reason is that? You dating someone new—"

"You lost the privilege to know what goes on in my life," she snapped.

A couple came out of the store nearest them. They cast curious gazes in their direction before continuing past them.

"Listen, I'm not trying to start an argument, Roxxy. I just want to talk to you." He slid forward quicker than Roxxy could react and gripped her shoulders. "I miss you. I miss us."

Her muscles stiffened. Gone were the feelings she'd had for him before. There used to be a day when his touch invited butteries to appear in her stomach. Now, there was a sour taste in her mouth. She could remember the day she'd walked in on him with that woman. Roxxy blinked, and the memory faded.

Images of Myles flashed before her, and his hands were the only ones she wanted on her.

"Well, you should have thought about us, before you got with her." She spun around on her heel but was snatched back by a strong hand on her forearm. Roxxy narrowed her eyes on Korey.

He had lost his mind if he thought he would be able to manhandle her.

"I want to know who you would be shopping for in there," he demanded, pointing at the lingerie store.

"None of your business," she ground out. She yanked her arm out of his gasp. "We're done here."

Roxxy turned on her heel and rushed to her car. She got in and slammed the door. Her gaze landed on Korey who stood before her car with his hands resting on his hips.

Her heart raced a mile a minute. She started the engine and threw the shift in reverse. She was livid.

How dare he try to act as if she had to answer to him about anything.

She tightened her grip on the steering wheel to keep her hands from trembling.

Her gaze flickered to the rearview mirror, and she prayed she didn't see Korey behind her.

The road was clear.

She breathed a sigh of relief.

Her cell rang, interrupting her thoughts.

Myles.

"Hello?" she answered, using her hands-free button on her steering wheel.

"What's wrong?" Myles replied immediately.

She smiled at the fierceness in his voice.

"It's nothing." She relaxed her hands on the steering wheel while the tension faded from her.

"It didn't sound like nothing when you answered the phone."

"I just ran into my ex, that's all. Just seeing him made the urge to commit murder rise up in me."

Myles gave a low chuckle. "Now as an officer of the law, I'm going to act like I didn't hear that."

"No, I wouldn't want you to be labeled as an accessory," she joked.

"The breakup was that bad?" he asked quietly.

"What would you think if you stopped by your boyfriend's house and found the waitress from ya'll favorite diner on her knees giving him head?"

"Ouch."

Roxxy grunted. "Exactly. He acts like I should have just forgiven him. The motherfucker even tried to blame me—" Roxxy caught herself.

She didn't want to go into details of her relationship with Korey. There was no point in her getting worked up over the past. She was happy with where she was and who she was currently fantasizing about all the time.

"You know what, I'm sorry," she breathed. She guided the vehicle to a halt at a stop light. Her gaze flickered to the mirror, and she was happy to see there was no sign of Korey. She'd half expected him to follow her.

"What's to be sorry for? Our past helps shape the person we are today," he replied. He gave a slight cough. "Plus, I'm reaping the reward for his mistake."

"You got that right," she muttered. The light

changed, and she pressed her foot down on the accelerator. It wouldn't take her long to get home now. The road opened up to a highway and the beautiful land of South Carolina. "So when can I bestow my gift upon you?"

Her heart missed a beat. He hadn't replied to her text, and she was already mortified that she was taking such brazen steps.

First sending the sexy picture to Myles, then boldly offering herself up to him.

"That's what I was calling for." His voice deepened.

She briefly closed her eyes, letting his baritone wash over her. She gripped the wheel tighter, imagining him next to her with his hands sliding down her body.

"I have a couple days off this week and figured if you could pencil me in on your busy sched—"

"When?" she asked, dancing in her seat. Her lips spread into a wide grin at his announcement.

"I could drive down tomorrow."

"You'd have to get a hotel." She bit her lip, hating how that sounded. She was a grown woman, but even at her age she didn't want to have the conversation with her parents about having a man stay over.

Plus, the noise they'd keep up, there was no way she'd be explaining that.

"I'm fine with that as long as you stay there with me."

"Um, did you think I wouldn't be staying with you?" She laughed. She immediately began thinking of all things she needed to pack.

Hell, with Myles, she was sure she'd only need her new slutty outfit she'd just purchased.

16

Myles glanced at his watch and was ready for this shift to be over. He'd be heading out first thing in the morning to go visit Roxxy. He couldn't wait to see her. Hearing her voice and seeing her on the screen was nothing compared to being able to feel her and breathe in her scent.

He walked through the precinct toward the conference room where they would be holding their interview with Officer Knight.

As with any potential new member joining the team, he'd looked into her and read her file. She was a generational cop. Her father had retired from Atlanta's police department. Her brother was a SWAT officer in Miami. Her grandfather had been a cop.

Policing was in her blood.

Already Myles had respect for her.

"Lover boy made it," Iker announced when Myles strolled through the door.

Today's meeting would be in the boardroom, not their usual conference room where they held their briefs.

Jokes flew through the air as he made his way to his seat. Zain, Brodie, Iker, Ash, and Declan were seated on the same side of table. The candidate would sit opposite the team where they could conduct their team interview.

"Whatever," he muttered. He sat back and glided a hand across his bald head.

"I hear you're taking a couple days off." Zain leaned over.

Myles glanced him. Zain's eyes twinkled, revealing his friend was up to something.

"Yeah, I am. I haven't had any real days off in a while." Myles shrugged.

"Going to go visit your girl?" Zain's lips grew into a grin.

"None of your damn business," Myles remarked. He tried to keep a straight face but he couldn't keep his lips from curving up into a small smile.

"Ahhh..." the guys teased and laughed.

Zain made the whipping sound.

"Fuck ya'll." Myles shook his head.

"Oh, how the mighty has fallen." Ash chuckled.

Declan coughed, obviously trying not to laugh. He

held up a hand. "Okay, men. We need to get serious for a second. We'll all talk about Myles in a bit."

The room quieted. A couple of snickers could be heard before the team turned their attention to Declan who stood from his seat.

"Mac is meeting with Officer Knight to explain the interviews to her. I'm sure I don't have to remind you to be professional with the questions. Did everyone review her CV?"

Nods went around.

Myles had to force himself to focus. He couldn't let Roxxy consume him now. Team interviews were essential. If the team was satisfied with the candidate, it could mean adding on to their team. It had been a few years since they'd accepted someone.

He tried to think if he had any questions for Knight. He was sure something would come to mind once they got the meeting going.

A few minutes later, Mac ushered Officer Knight into the room. She was an African-American woman, tall and fit. Her dark hair was pulled back away from her face in a respectable ponytail. Her face was void of any emotions, making it hard for Myles to read her. She took her seat and gave a tight smile to the room.

"Officer Knight, I'm sure you have met the team, but I'll go around and introduce everyone," Mac began.

He moved over to the corner. He announced each man's name to move the introductions quickly.

"It's nice to formally meet everyone," Jordan said. She had good eye contact with them.

Myles was pleased. Meeting their team sometimes caused anxiety or the candidate to become flustered.

Jordan, on the other hand, was cool as a cucumber.

"Thanks for applying for SWAT. We reviewed your file and see you were with Atlanta's PD for some time. Why the transfer?" Declan started the questions off.

Jordan sat back and crossed her legs. She was still dressed in her blues, but she appeared as if she were in comfortable clothing.

"My sister lives here in Columbia. She recently became a widow and now is a single mom to two rambunctious boys. She needed me, and I was willing to move here to be close to her so I could help out."

Loyal to family. That was a good quality and one that was needed for a SWAT officer.

The level of respect for her was rising.

"What makes you the best candidate out of all the ones who applied?" Zain asked.

The room was dead quiet and slightly tense. This was the one time that the team came together to assess the candidates, and they had to nail the interview.

"Police work is all I know. My father was a cop. My

brother is SWAT for Miami. My grandfather was a cop, as was his father. I grew up surrounded by policemen and women. I've always had a great respect SWAT officers. I feel that I am the best to join this team, because I know what it takes to be a member. Long days and nights, physically fit to be able to do the job, intelligence, discipline, skills, and camaraderie. You can check with any of the partners I've had in the past, and they will vouch that I have all of that."

Myles had to fight back a grin. She was spunky. The woman obviously knew what it would take to be on their team.

"Training. How have you trained? You impressed us at tryouts, hence why you are here, but what have you done in the past that gives you an edge?" Iker asked.

A grin spread. "Being one of few women gave me the drive to ensure I am the best at what I do. In Atlanta I always felt I had to prove myself because of who my father is and because I'm a woman. So I've trained with the Atlanta guys and with my brother's team when I would visit him. Not only am I a master of weapons, but I hold a black belt in karate."

"Why didn't you try out for Atlanta before you moved?" Brodie asked.

"The year before I came here, my sister's husband was very ill. I couldn't commit to what they needed at the time because my priority was my sister and her family." Jordan's gaze landed on Myles.

He had yet to ask a question. He had been studying her the entire time. Watching her body language.

To sum it up, the woman bled blue. She was a tough cookie and fiercely loyal to her family.

"What do you hope to get out of joining SWAT?" Myles asked. He knew why most people wanted to, but there was something that everyone wanted out of the special team they applied for.

Being SWAT didn't make a person rich by any means. The job would beat that person down and take everything from them.

Jordan stared at Myles. She blinked a few times. It wasn't a normal question to ask, but her answer would be the determining factor for Myles.

"What do I hope to gain from joining SWAT?" she repeated the question back. Her brow furrowed while she thought of her answer. "That's a good question, Officer Burton. Besides the opportunity to use my skills, I would say a team where I would really feel like I belong."

Myles sat back.

He was satisfied with the answer.

The interview lasted another twenty minutes until

the guys reached a place where they felt they had asked all the questions they needed.

"Let me walk you out," Mac offered. He pushed off the wall since the team had concluded their interview. "Thanks for coming at the end of your shift. We appreciate it."

Jordan stood with a smile. "It was no problem. Thank you, gentlemen. I really appreciate the opportunity to sit down and speak with you. Have a good evening."

"Have a good one." Myles nodded to her.

She turned on her heel and exited with Mac behind her. The room remained silent as each man pondered over the interview.

Myles knew his answer.

Mac returned and shut the door. He stood next to the chair Jordan had vacated. He met each member's gaze.

"All those in favor of Officer Knight moving forward, say aye," he commanded, not beating around the bush.

"Aye." Replies echoed through the room.

The team had made their decision.

Officer Knight could move on to the next phase of interviews.

Roxxy glanced around her room to double-check if she was forgetting to pack anything.

Two nights in town with Myles had her nervous.

What if he got bored in their little town—

"Wait a darn minute. He's going to be with me. There won't be any time for him to get bored."

What was she thinking?

A knock sounded at her door.

"Come in!" she called out. She turned and zipped up her small suitcase.

"Are you going to let us meet your friend?" a deep voice asked from behind her.

Roxxy flew around to find her father standing in her doorway. Her face warmed instantly. She had hoped he was going to be gone all day.

Roxxy didn't know why, with one glance from her father, she felt fourteen again.

"Of course. Did you think I was going to just sneak out the house?" She forced a laugh. She brushed past him and walked toward the stairs.

"You've done that a time or two before." He chuckled. He followed her down to the first floor.

Her mother hummed, and Roxxy followed the sound.

Shelby was in the kitchen fixing lunch. This was safer ground to have this conversation. She'd rather have her mom in the room.

"What time is your gentleman caller arriving?" Shelby asked.

Roxxy rolled her eyes as she took a seat at the island. "Mom, this is not the ninetieth century."

"Well, what am I to call him? Is he your boyfriend?" Shelby rested her hands on her hips.

"How about we back up to what is the young man's name?" Earl asked. He walked over to his wife and placed a kiss on her cheek.

Shelby melted against him with a small giggle.

Roxxy sighed. She hoped to one day have what her parents had.

Earl turned his attention to her.

Roxxy blew out a deep breath. She might as well get this over with.

"His name is Myles Burton," she blurted out.

Her father's eyebrows shot up. "Really." He folded his arms across his chest and stared at her.

She swallowed hard, knowing what he was thinking.

That morning at the hotel when he saw Myles leaving their hotel in Columbia.

"I asked you if you knew why Burton was coming from the elevator—"

"Oh, hush up, Earl." Shelby swatted her husband's arm. "Leave the girl be. There are some things she's not going to fess up to with her father."

His brow furrowed, and he turned to Shelby. "But, honey—"

"Oh, don't you 'honey' me. I remember a time when a certain young man was caught crawling out my bedroom window."

Roxxy burst out laughing. This was one story she had yet to hear from her parents.

Imagine that.

Earl Sutton had got caught sneaking out her mother's bedroom window.

"My daddy had his shotgun. You should have seen your daddy sprint across the field to where his truck was parked." Shelby had tears running down her face.

Earl shook his head and held his hands up. "I give up."

Roxxy wiped the tears from her cheeks. She hopped down from the chair and walked over to her father. She wrapped her arms around his waist. He rested his arm around her shoulders and hugged her back.

"It's okay, Daddy. Myles is a good man. You would like him. He's an Army man like yourself."

"I heard." Earl instantly warmed up.

Roxxy knew her father, and he was loyal to his Army men. That would be one thing that he and Myles could bond over.

Earl placed a kiss on Roxxy's forehead. "If he hurts

you, I don't care what branch he served in. My bullets aren't prejudiced at all."

"Oh, you hush now. From what Roxxy tells me, he's a fine, standup man. I can't wait to meet him," Shelby announced. She turned back to her task of sandwich making.

"So you've already shared with your mother about Burton?" her father asked.

Roxxy slipped away and walked to the fridge. Before she left with Myles, she had planned to take him riding up to her favorite spot. They would have lunch out on the farm. She wanted to show him where she lived and give her big city man a taste of the country.

She had to introduce him to her mare, Sunshine. That horse was considered a best friend of Roxxy's. She'd had her forever, and it was important that her two special people meet.

"You know how us girls gossip." Shelby placed the sandwiches in a container. She had agreed to make lunch for Roxxy and Myles. Shelby Sutton's cooking was known all over the county. A few things had rubbed off on Roxxy, but today, she was treating Myles to Shelby's food.

"What time is he going to arrive?" Earl asked, leaning against the counter.

They were interrupted by the sound of the doorbell. Roxxy grinned and fought back jumping in place like a young schoolgirl. She was a grown woman and should be acting like it.

But the memories of riding Myles's thick cock dried her mouth.

"Now. Promise me you will be behave." She gave her father the same stare he gave her when he meant business.

"Of course he will." Her mother elbowed her father in the side. "Go on, girl. Don't leave your man out there waiting."

Roxxy grinned, not needing to be told twice. She turned on her heel and practically ran to the front door.

She paused in the foyer and tried to will her heart to slow down. Glancing at the mirror on the wall, she made sure she appeared perfect. Satisfied with her appearance, she stepped back and strolled to the door.

She opened it, and there was Myles, larger than life. He looked even better than the last time they'd FaceTimed each other, which was last night. The sight of him in a tight t-shirt, jeans, and boots had her core clenching.

Damn, this man is sexy as sin.

He had a bouquet of flowers in his hands.

Roxxy melted.

She was a sucker for roses.

"Hi there," she drawled.

"Hey."

His gaze slid down her body, sending a chill down her spine. She knew that expression. If her parents weren't home, she'd drag him up to her room so she could have her way with him.

"These are for you." He handed them to her.

There was a mix of pink, red, and yellow roses. Roxxy leaned down and sniffed them.

She sighed.

She was falling for this big hunk of a man.

No question about it, Myles Burton had snuck inside her heart.

"They are beautiful," she whispered. She stepped forward.

He immediately gripped her hips, closing the gap between them. She stood on tiptoe and offered her lips to him. He didn't hesitate in swooping down to claim them.

He commanded the kiss. She had no issues submitting to him while he thoroughly kissed her to within an inch of her life.

They pulled back from each other. Roxxy's breaths were coming fast. Her body ached for him, but there was nothing they could do now.

Hell, his rock-hard dick was brushing against her stomach. Fifteen, no, ten minutes was all she needed with him just to take this ache away. Memories of the feel and taste of him in her mouth had her licking her lips.

Down, girl. There will be plenty of time for that later.

"I wasn't sure what type of flowers you liked," he admitted sheepishly.

Roxxy laughed and stepped back. She entwined her fingers with his. "They are perfect and just so happen to be my favorite."

"Good, because I can't ever remember buying flowers before." He laughed. He ran a hand over his head and stared at her.

Her heartbeat flickered out of time. His admission was important. If this was new to him, then he was definitely taking what they had between them seriously.

"Let me take you in to meet my parents." She had totally forgotten they were waiting on them.

"Okay. Then what's this great plan you had?" he asked. He gave her a suspicious look.

Last night she had admitted she wanted to plan their first day together and would make all the arrangements.

She leaned into him and pressed a kiss to his chin. "We're going riding, city boy."

17

Myles was going to be sore in the morning. It had been years since he'd been on top of a horse. Hell, the last time was in the Army. He and his team had been deployed in some remote areas of Kuwait that would only allow them to travel by horses.

He'd had a crash course in riding then, and it appeared like today was going to be his crash course refresher.

Roxxy, on the other hand, was a natural. She looked as if she were born to ride. Her long hair flowed behind her, and her small cowgirl hat was adorable on her.

But he couldn't take his eyes off the way she was perched in the saddle and how she moved as one with the mare.

His mind was immediately thinking dirty thoughts.

Tonight, his Roxxy would be sitting astride him just like that.

Only she'd be naked, and his cock would be buried deep inside her while she rode him.

"Come on, slowpoke. Midnight won't hurt you," Roxxy called out over her shoulder.

"We're still getting to know each other," he replied. The horse beneath him was beautiful and had the silkiest black coat he'd ever seen.

Midnight was the perfect name for him.

Myles breathed in the fresh air. Coming down here had been a good idea. Getting away from the hustle and bustle of city life and crime was just what he needed.

The meeting of her parents had gone well. Shelby Sutton was the exact image of Roxxy. The older woman had immediately welcomed him with open arms and one hell of a hug. Her smile was infectious, and it was easy to see why Earl Sutton had fallen for the woman.

Earl was more withdrawn, but of course he should be. The man was meeting his daughter's lover...eh... boyfriend. Myles liked the sound of that. He had never been one to commit to a woman before, but never had he met one like Roxxy. She was one of a kind.

"Come, boy. We can't let the women show us up." Myles urged the horse on. He was caught up in the beauty of the land. The grass was bright green, and the woods they were nearing was plush and overgrown.

Roxxy turned around and tossed him a wink. She pointed to an area up ahead. "We're almost there. See that tree over there where the hill starts? That's where we're going."

Myles nodded, thankful they were almost at their destination. He held on to the reins and was glad Midnight was mild-mannered and followed Roxxy. Hanging on by a thread on a runaway horse wouldn't be a cool look for him.

Ten minutes later, Roxxy did a perfect dismount. Myles watched, envious. He hoped he was half as graceful as Roxxy when he got down.

"You need help?" Roxxy asked, petting her mare.

Her gaze turned to him, and he shook his head.

"Me? Need help?" He waved a hand at her. "I got this."

"Oh, okay." The doubt on her face didn't sit well for his manly pride.

He'd show her.

He'd got on the damn horse by himself, he would be getting off on his own.

He tossed his leg over and attempted to slide off Midnight.

Wrong move.

The animal stepped to the side as he promptly fell on his ass.

"Thanks, Midnight," he muttered.

Midnight nickered as if to reply.

"Are you okay?" Roxxy rushed to his side. She knelt on the ground next to him, obviously holding back a smile.

"Yeah, I'm okay." His lips tilted in the corners. "Just my pride is bruised along with my ass."

Roxxy fell into a fit of laughter. She tilted over and landed on him. Myles gave in and chuckled with her.

The sound of her giggles floated through the air, and Myles vowed he'd always try to make sure she had a reason to laugh.

Just not anything that would cause pain to him. He was definitely going to be sore in the morning.

He rolled them over, landing on top of her. The grass was thick, but it certainly didn't cushion his fall too well.

"So that was funny, huh?" he growled. He pushed her arms over her head.

"I'm sorry," she hiccuped. Tears escaped her eyes while giggles still escaped her.

"I got you." He gripped her wrists in one hand and slid his free one down her side and gave her a little tickle.

She howled and tried to buck him off her. Her laughter grew until screams escaped her.

"Uncle!" she cried while kicking her legs.

Myles released her. Her chest was rising and

falling fast while she tried to catch her breath. He stared down into her beautiful eyes. She quieted, and they just gazed at each other.

He trailed a hand over her face, wiping the wetness from her skin.

"I don't want to give you a big head or anything, but I did miss you," she whispered.

"I missed you, too." He leaned down and pressed a chaste peck to her lips.

How did he think he was going to be satisfied with just one kiss?

He covered her mouth with his again. Roxxy released a moan while encircling his neck with her arms to bring him close to her. He took advantage of just them out in nature to properly kiss her the way he had been wanting to.

He hardened, but now wasn't the time. Myles lifted his head to find Midnight grazing near them. The horse was curiously observing them while he munched on the grass.

"Are you hungry?" Roxxy asked. Her lips were swollen from their kiss.

"Yeah. I'm famished."

Not for food.

He needed Roxxy.

Myles wasn't ready to perform with a nosey horse standing next to them.

"We will finish this later," he promised. He pushed off the ground and held out a hand for Roxxy.

"I'm counting on it." Her smaller hand slipped into his.

He hefted her up onto her feet. She stumbled and landed against him. He released a groan at the feel of her.

"Momma's cooking is famous." Roxxy patted his abdomen. She reached up and pressed a kiss to his chin. "Come on so I can feed my man."

She rotated and walked back to Sunshine. His gaze dropped down to her ass.

He adjusted himself in his jeans. Roxxy turned and caught him staring at her. She tossed him wink.

Busted, but he didn't care.

It was a fine ass.

"What about the them?" Myles glanced at Midnight who didn't have a care in the world. Myles was impressed how trained they were.

"Take his reins and bring him over here. We can let them graze while we eat."

"Come on, boy," he murmured. He took the leather straps and guided the horse over to where Roxxy and Sunshine stood.

Roxxy pulled out a large blanket from her saddlebag and handed it to him. "Spread that out for me, sweetie."

They worked together to get their picnic set up. Myles took in all of the food Mrs. Sutton had packed away for them.

"Are we expecting company?" he joked, sitting on the blanket next to Roxxy.

"My mom tends to go overboard a little." Roxxy chuckled. She reached inside a cooler bag and brought out wrapped sandwiches.

Myles hadn't realized how hungry he was until he saw the food spread out in front of them. His stomach growled.

"Here are some cold-cut sandwiches. I don't know what she does to these things, but they are addictive."

She handed him one. The six-inch sandwich was filled with meat and all of the fixings. They had potato salad, fruit, brownies, and a thermos of iced sweet tea. Mrs. Sutton had certainly outdone herself.

They ate in a comfortable silence.

Roxxy was right. Her mother did something magical to the sandwiches. Her potato salad was like no other one he'd had before. The iced tea was just what he was expecting from a southerner.

Sweet enough to give a person diabetes.

"The land is gorgeous," he commented in between bites.

"It is. This is my favorite area. It's like a little hide-away, but I'm still able to look out on everything." She took a sip of her tea before turning to him. "I've been coming to this spot since I was a kid. Whenever I needed to be alone and gather my thoughts, I'd come here."

Myles wiped his mouth with his napkin. He reached for her hand and brought it up to his lips.

"Thanks for sharing your special spot with me," he murmured. It really meant a lot to him. She didn't have to bring him to her little oasis, but she'd chosen to share it with him.

Seeing her on the horse and out in the country let him see the real Roxxy.

She wasn't just the hard-nosed auditor she portrayed back in Columbia. Here she could just be herself.

"Eat up. Momma will be insulted if we don't put a bigger dent in this food." Roxxy waved to the spread.

Myles patted his flat stomach and nodded. "Yes, ma'am."

He didn't want to disappoint Mrs. Sutton.

They finished what they could and put away the leftovers they didn't make it to.

Myles laid back on the makeshift pillow of the bags. It wasn't the most comfortable, but it allowed him to let Roxxy to snuggle up against him.

They watched the clouds and just talked.

Myles had never felt so comfortable around a

woman before. They spoke of their childhoods and anything that came to mind.

Even the periods of quietness were nice.

Just lying under the big blue sky with his woman next to him.

That was all Myles really needed.

"Look at that cloud!" Roxxy pointed. Excitement lined her voice. "It's a snowman."

"What? A snowman?" He squinted slightly. He could sort of see it, but not really. "I don't know. Look at that one. It resembles a skater."

"A skater? How do you see that?" Roxxy snickered. She leaned up and rested on her elbow. Her long dark hair fell around her shoulders while she stared at him.

Her beauty always captivated him. Myles reached up and tucked her hair behind her ear. He couldn't read her expression. Her gaze dropped down to his lips.

"What is it?" he asked.

"Nothing," she whispered.

"It doesn't seem like nothing."

"I'm just happy," she admitted. She pressed a kiss to his lips. "I'm enjoying our time together."

He slid his hand to the base of her neck and brought her back to him. He kissed her again.

"I'm having a good time, too," he said.

She pushed off the ground and straddled him. She

moved his pillow out of the way and held his arms over his head.

Myles let her be in control. If he wanted to, he could move her, but he'd play her little game and let her have her fun.

"Don't move," she murmured.

"Why not?" His eyebrow rose.

"And no questions." She gave a cute growl. She leaned over and kissed him again.

"Yes, ma'am." He chuckled.

She slid his hands down his chest and stopped them at the edge of his shaft. His breath caught in his throat at the twinkle in her eyes.

Roxxy pulled his shirt up and got it stuck on his head.

"Help me," she breathed.

"You told me not to move—"

"Myles!" She giggled. "Okay. You can only move when I tell you to."

He shifted and tugged the shirt over his head and dropped it down on the blanket next to him.

"Stubborn man," she muttered.

"I told you I always follow orders," he teased.

He breathed in sharply the second her tongue touched his nipple. She trailed it down his chest and south to the ridges of his abdomen.

"Really? Well, we're going to test that out today."

She glanced up at him and winked. Her hands slowly made their way to his belt. They paused, resting there while she placed a small kiss on the lower part of his stomach. "Promise me you won't move?"

"I won't. What do you have in mind?"

She slid the belt from under the metal clasp.

"Oh, I know of something you might like." The button popped free. The sound of the zipper cut through the air. Her gaze moved to his jeans as she concentrated on removing them.

"Is that so?"

"Yep."

His shoes and jeans joined his shirt in a growing pile.

"What about your clothes?" He lay there on the blanket in nothing but his boxer briefs. His cock was straining against the cotton material, forming a tent.

Roxxy sat back with a grin. She ripped her shirt over her head and discarded her shorts.

Myles's mouth went dry at the sight of her perfect brown skin in the sunlight. Her dark hair flowed over her naked shoulders. She was left in a sheer bra and panty matching set, and Myles wished he had a camera to take a picture. It was a sight he would want to keep forever.

"Happy now?" Her hand skimmed his thigh and traced up to his dick. She gripped it in her hand, the underwear the only barrier between her smooth skin and his hard shaft.

"No," he responded through clenched teeth.

She bit her lip while she worked on bringing him out through the slit in his boxers.

Myles's head fell back at the sensation of her smooth hands running up his length. A groan escaped him.

Her lips wrapped around the head of his cock.

His lungs burned, needing air, but he was left breathless when she sucked him farther into her mouth.

"Roxxy." He gripped her hair while she continued her task. The pleasure built up in his chest as she took her time worshipping his cock.

There was no other way to describe what she did when she had him in her mouth.

The woman certainly loved to suck his dick, and he was not going to take away her favorite pastime.

Her slight moans fueled his desire for her.

The pressure was building in his scrotum.

Roxxy added both of her hands to travel his length while her mouth enveloped him.

"Roxxy, girl," he groaned. His stomach clenched. He needed to hold on to something, but his hand was only met with the blanket that rested beneath him.

"Don't worry. I won't be gone long." She tossed him a wink and walked away. She put a little more sway in her hips with the knowledge that he was still watching her. She took the two steps up to where the host stood. "Excuse me. Where is the ladies' room?"

"Down this hallway. You'll find it on the left." He smiled at her.

"Thanks." She followed his directions and found her destination. She pushed open the door and stepped into the lavatory. It was tastefully decorated with rich deep colors. There was a small sitting area before the row of private stalls.

Roxxy quickly handled her business and washed her hands. She stared at herself in the mirror and almost didn't recognize herself.

She looked radiant. Happy. A crooked grin was evident.

All because of Myles.

He was like a breath of fresh air. She was his main focus, and she liked being the center of attention for once.

Roxxy took an extra minute to reapply her lipstick and comb through her hair. Her black dress fit her perfect. Myles's eyes had lit up when she'd put it on. A shiver slid down her spine at the thought of him taking it off later.

She threw her lipstick and comb back into her

purse. She gave herself one last quick look over and found herself to be flawless.

She spun on her heel and exited the bathroom. Her heels clicked on the marble floor. Her gaze lifted, and her breath froze in place.

"Roxxy, we need to talk." Korey stood before her. He was dressed in his infamous jeans and a plaid long-sleeved cotton button-down.

"Korey, I don't have anything to say to you." She folded her arms in front of her.

How the hell did he know where she was?

"Look, I know I messed up. Let's talk about—"

"First off, messed up is too light of a phrase for what you did to me," she snapped. "I'm done. We've been done."

She moved to brush past him, but he yanked her arm. A gasp escaped her. He turned her around to face him. His eyes narrowed on her. His nostrils flared as he took in her outfit.

"Who are you here with, Roxxy? You think you can just replace me so easily?" he bit out.

"Aren't you the pot calling the kettle black. You had no problems replacing me." She wasn't going to hold any punches with him. She had thought he'd ruined her. Broken her heart, but now, she was thankful she was able to see his true colors. If he hadn't, her life would be different now. "Let me go."

"Roxxy—"

"You must have a hearing problem," a deep voice growled from behind Roxxy.

She froze in place. She knew that voice, only this time it was cold, and the hairs on her arms rose.

Myles.

She glanced over her shoulder, and his fierce gaze was locked on Korey. Myles had about three inches on Korey and about thirty pounds of muscle on him, too.

This was a side of Myles she'd never seen before.

The hard glint in his eyes and the firm set of his jaw was a direct warning that he was pissed.

"Who the hell is this?" Korey snarled. He tightened his grip on Roxxy's arm.

"The man who's going to break your hand if you don't take it off Roxxy." Myles's voice was calm but held a deadly vibe to it.

Korey's grip on her lightened. She snatched her arm away. She automatically moved closer to Myles.

"Listen here, buddy. I don't know who you think you are, but this doesn't concern you." Korey dismissed Myles.

"Anything to do with Roxxy concerns me." Myles positioned himself in front of her. He was now between her and Korey.

Roxxy had to peek around Myles's muscular form. Korey had a scowl on his face.

He wasn't happy.

Too bad.

"Is that so? Fucked her a few times? She's a good lay, isn't she?" Korey taunted.

A deep growl rumbled from Myles. Roxxy flew forward and snagged his arm. She tugged back with all her strength. It was like trying to stop a pissed-off grizzly bear. They were drawing a crowd, and she didn't want Korey to get his ass kicked in such a nice fancy place.

Outside, that was another thing.

"Myles, he's not worth it," she pleaded. She pulled on him, but he didn't budge.

"It's okay, Roxxy girl. I just wanted to make sure I heard him straight." Myles shrugged off her hold on him and stepped in front of Korey.

The two of them squared off.

Roxxy looked around. She prayed no one had called the police.

On second thought, she hoped they did. There was no way she was going to be able to break up the two of them if they came to blows.

"I'm not scared of you," Korey sneered. His gaze didn't waver from Myles. "And you heard what I said. Having fun sleeping with my woman?"

"I'm going to say this once. Stay away from Roxxy.

She's no longer your concern." Myles's voice was clipped.

"Is there a problem over here?"

Roxxy glanced over her shoulder. The host was standing there with a waiter. Their watchful eyes were on Myles and Korey.

"No problem, gentlemen. I was just leaving." Korey brushed past Myles.

His dark gaze slammed into Roxxy, sending a chill down her spine. She straightened to her full height and returned his look.

He strode forward toward the two men. "It was just a misunderstanding, but it's been clarified." He patted the host on the shoulder and disappeared around the corner.

"Everything's okay," Roxxy noted. She didn't wait for a response before she turned back to Myles. She stepped toward him.

His chest was rising and falling quickly. His hands were curled into tight fists.

Roxxy laid a gentle hand on his chest.

His eyes dropped down to her.

"Are you all right?" His voice was gruff. He reached up and cupped her cheek in his warm hand.

She smiled softly. "I am now."

"I didn't like the way he was touching you," Myles

admitted. He reached for her and brought her flush against him.

"Me neither. Thank you for coming to my aid." She tried to laugh at the situation, but it sounded strained to her ears.

"If he bothers you again when I'm not here, you just say—"

"I'll be fine. I can handle Korey." She slid her hand up his chest. He didn't look convinced. She rolled her eyes. "I always have a weapon somewhere on me or in my car."

That seemed to satisfy him. He jerked his head in a nod.

"Want to go back and order dessert?" Myles appeared to calm down slightly.

Roxxy shook her head. "No, let's take care of the check and go."

Myles's gaze swept the lot as he and Roxxy made their way to his car. He tried to settle the rage inside him but he was having a hard time. His gut was screaming that someone had their eyes on him. Ever since he'd arrived in town the same feeling had stayed with him.

"Hey, why don't we get dessert after all?" Roxxy paused.

"What do you have in mind?" he asked.

Her smile spread across her face. He wished he could relax as fast as she could, but Roxxy wasn't a trained soldier.

He glanced around again, his gaze sweeping the area.

"What are you looking for?" Roxxy turned around and eyed at the area. Her eyebrows rose high.

"It's nothing." He tugged her close to him.

She studied him for a brief moment before she leaned into him. "Well, the place I have in mind is a short distance away. We can leave the car here and walk." She patted his chest.

Memories of how that ass had gripped her wrist came to mind. Myles snagged her hand and brought it up to where he could assess it. In the low light, he couldn't see any marks on her.

Had Korey put one blemish on Roxxy's flawless skin, Myles wouldn't have been responsible for his actions.

"Do you want to talk about what happened back there?" he asked.

Roxxy shook her head. "He's harmless. I just want to forget it and enjoy what's left of our date."

By her facial expression, Myles decided to leave it be for now, but he was not one to let anything like that be forgotten.

They strolled down the street with light conversation. Roxxy told him stories of each storefront. He listened but constantly scanned the area.

The night sky was clear with a few clouds. Parked cars lined road, and there were a couple pedestrians on the opposite side of the street.

"You will love Charlie's ice cream. It's homemade, and you can have whatever toppings you crave. What's your favorite flavor of ice cream?" she asked.

They paused outside Charlie's Chocolate Shop. Myles glanced at the rustic building with cow decals on the window.

"Well, I'm known somewhat as an expert on ice cream." He pulled her in closer to him.

She turned in his arms with a smile and giggle. "Is that so?"

"Oh, yes. Not only am I an expert on weapons and being able to shoot at abnormally long ranges, but I have a complete knowledge of the different flavors of ice cream."

Roxxy barked a hearty laugh.

The sound of an engine revving caught his attention. He casually peeked over Roxxy's shoulder and caught sight of a dark sedan at the intersection a half a block away.

His muscles tensed.

Something wasn't right.

"Come on. Let's go in." Roxxy grabbed his hand and tugged him toward the door.

Once inside, he relaxed slightly. The shop was cozy and unrefined. The walls were open brick, the floors hardwood, and the tables matched the floors with two-tone wood. They walked over to the counter and were able to view the different flavors of ice cream behind the glass protector.

"Hi. Can I help you?" a young teenage girl asked.

Her hair was drawn up in a high ponytail, and the glimmer of silver on her teeth reminded Myles of his youth when he had to wear braces. He offered her a smile.

"What's your favorite?" he asked.

Roxxy stood with her face practically pressed to the glass while she browsed.

"You look as if you love to live dangerously." The girl paused with her finger on her chin.

His gaze dropped down to her name tag. Lindsey.

"Really?" His eyebrows rose. This young girl would make one hell of a profiler to be able to pick up on his nature so quickly.

"Yup. You like to try things." She laughed.

"That I do." He chuckled. "Hit me with your recommendation, Lindsey."

19

Roxxy knew Myles was hiding something from her. His eyes were always moving, assessing as they'd walked down the street toward the ice cream shop. It was the soldier in him, she'd seen the look before.

But there was something more.

Myles tossed their trash away. She stood from her seat and grabbed her purse.

"Ready?" Myles asked.

She nodded and walked over to him. Their dessert date had gone just as planned.

No one could stay angry while eating ice cream.

"Yes," she breathed. She took his outstretched hand in hers.

Myles opened the door and escorted her outside.

"I was thinking when we return to the hotel, me and you will have some fun in the jacuzzi," she said.

"I like the sound of that." Myles's deep laugh rumbled in his chest.

She stood and turned to Myles. "Are you crazy?" she shouted.

He grimaced and held a hand to his shoulder. Her gaze dropped down to his hand. His fingers were stained red.

"Oh my God. You've been shot!" she cried out. Her hand flew to him to help staunch the flow of blood.

"I'll be fine. It went straight through," he gritted out through clenched teeth.

"You need a hospital," she snapped.

People began milling out of the storefronts, looking around in disbelief. The sound of sirens echoed through the air. They grew louder as time passed.

"We need to get out of here." Myles brushed past her.

She stared after him with her mouth hanging open. Seeing that he wasn't slowing down, she took off after him.

"Why the hell can't I take you to the hospital?" She walked next to him.

"I don't like hospitals," he muttered.

They veered into the lot where he'd parked his vehicle.

"You're going to have to drive," he said.

She swung around on him. "Who was that?"

"How the hell do I know? I didn't get the chance to

ask them when they were spraying us with their bullets."

They stood still, staring at each other. Roxxy didn't know what to think.

"Are you sure?"

"Could that have been lover boy?" He cocked an eyebrow.

"Korey?" She gasped. She shook her head fiercely. "He's a rancher, not a gangster, and certainly not a killer."

"Does the rancher know how to use a gun?" he asked, stepping toward her.

Roxxy stood her ground and placed her hands on her hips. "Of course he does. Everyone in this town knows how to shoot a gun!" she practically yelled.

Myles paused. He closed his eyes briefly and reached inside his pants pocket. "Here. You drive."

"Back to the hotel?" she asked.

He opened the driver's door for her and helped her get in. He shut it and walked to the passenger side.

He slammed the door and leaned his chair back.

"Well?" She started the car and turned to him.

"No. Your place."

Roxxy's nerves were shot. The entire drive back to her

house was tense. Her gaze kept going to the review mirror to make sure they weren't followed. She felt as if she had dived face forward into some cop drama television show.

She guided the car onto the gravel driveway that led to the main house.

"Drive around to the barn," Myles said softly.

She practically jumped out of her skin. He hadn't spoken in a while, leaving Roxxy to assume he'd dozed off.

Roxxy glanced at him and found his eyes to be closed. Her heart pounded, and she feared he had lost too much blood. There was a slight copper scent in the air that worried her.

"Are you okay?" she whispered.

"Me? Of course I am. Nothing like a little graze would take me down."

"Graze? Myles, there was blood running down your entire arm. I'd say that was more than a graze."

He waved a hand in the air. "I've had much worse."

She gripped the steering wheel tight at his comment. She didn't even want to imagine what that meant. He'd spent time in the Army and had been on SWAT for years. She knew his background. Both of his jobs were extremely dangerous, and she'd be ignorant if she thought he would be able get through either unscathed.

"Well, let's not test it. I still think you should be at the hospital," she muttered.

The main house came into view. She did as Myles instructed and drove around back to the barn. She brought them to a halt and cut the engine off.

"Why the barn?" she asked.

Myles opened his eyes. In the darkness she could see his grin.

"I may not be originally from the south, but my momma taught me manners. No dripping blood over a woman's floors." He opened his door and got out.

Roxxy couldn't help but giggle. She exited and followed him into the barn.

"Really? You're afraid of messing up my mother's floors with your blood?" she asked.

He paused at the door of the barn and turned to her.

"Do you think she'd care—"

"No. Whoever that was who shot at us, they wanted us dead. My gut feeling is that they are going to come for us. I figured our best bet would be here on your family's land than stuck in some hotel room without a clear path of escape."

Roxxy froze in place. The grimness of his words rocked her to her core.

They are going to come for us.

"Um, okay." Roxxy didn't know what else to say.

She ran a shaky hand through her hair, trying to get her brain to wake up. "Who is going to come for us? What the hell is going on?"

Finally, her brain kicked in.

"I'm not sure, but we are certainly going to find out," Myles replied grimly.

"Come on. Let's get you inside." She opened the door to the barn and guided Myles inside.

There was a room off in the corner. It was a makeshift office for the ranch hands. Roxxy flipped on the light and waved to the small couch.

"Have a seat. I'll be right back." She tossed her purse on the desk then left. She quickly made her way to the bathroom. They'd had it installed so the hands could have facilities to use and could get washed up before eating. Running a farm was dirty work. This lavatory in the barn had been a great investment.

She grabbed the first-aid kit from under the sink as well as a few other items and rushed back to the office. Myles was perched on the edge of the desk while speaking into his cell phone.

"I need you to run a plate for me." His eyes met hers.

She signaled for him to remove his shirt. She set the kit down on the desk and opened it. She took out the prepackaged gauze and antiseptic ointment.

Turning back to him, she saw he would need

assistance in taking the shirt off.

"I'll do it," she murmured. Roxxy stood before him and brushed his hand out of the way. She reached up and began undoing the buttons. Had this been any other day and Myles wasn't bleeding, she would turn this into a playful strip tease.

"South Carolina. License plate number is TGB 84T."

Roxxy got to the bottom and had to pull his shirt from out of his waistband. Her gaze landed on the bulge in his pants then flew up and met Myles's.

He shrugged his good shoulder.

She rolled her eyes and helped take the shirt off him as gently as she could. He grimaced when he had to lift the arm that was hit by the bullet.

"Reported stolen three days ago." Myles paused, apparently listening to the person on the other end of the line. "All right. Hit me back when you got something. Thanks, man." He disconnected the call and placed his phone on the desk.

"Nothing?" she asked.

"I figured the car would be stolen. Only idiots would use their car to do crimes."

"I'm sure there are a few out there..." She trailed off.

"You wouldn't even begin to imagine the stories I could tell." He chuckled.

"Tell me some," she encouraged. She had to find something to occupy her thoughts. Myles standing before her in a bright-white tank that highlighted his deep complexion and muscles had her libido running wild. She reached for a couple of the gauzes and ripped the protective paper cover open.

"When I first joined the department, there was a string of bank robberies. I was a beat cop fresh on the force." He paused, grimacing as she poured some rubbing alcohol on the wound. "Jesus, you could have warned me."

"You may not have let me had I told you." She chuckled and blotted the wound with the clean gauze. "Don't tell me this is too painful for you."

"Just warn me." He blinked a few times.

"Go the hospital," she retorted. "Or how about, not get shot."

"Anyway." He blew out a deep breath. "We got the call of a robbery in progress. By the time my partner and I arrived at the bank, the bad guys had hopped into a Buick and sped off. It was the same car that had been spotted at two other bank robberies. We immediately began to give chase. The guys drove to a church and jumped out and took off on foot."

"A church?" she questioned.

Myles released a hiss when she held a clean cloth to his wound. He was right. It had gone straight through him. It wasn't large, but for some reason he'd bled like it had been. "Hold this in place," she instructed.

Myles reached up with his good hand and held the dressing.

"Apparently, the idiots had borrowed their grandmother's car to rob the banks and would drop her car off to her while she was worshipping."

"What?" Roxxy barked a laugh. She took the tape that came in the kit and wrapped it around Myles's biceps a few times to create a bandage. She tore the tape and patted it down to stay put. "There you go."

"Thanks," he murmured, his dark eyes locked with hers.

She placed the tape on the desk and rested her hands on his chest. He pulled her closer between his open legs.

"I don't like knowing you're hurt." She pouted slightly.

It was the truth. Seeing him get shot replayed over in her mind repeatedly.

"I don't like that someone was shooting at you." He reached up and cupped her cheek.

She leaned into it, loving the feel of his warmth.

"You were there to protect me," she whispered. She slid her hands up his chest so they made their way to his neck.

Myles pulled her flush against him and lowered his head. He pressed his lips to hers. She sighed and parted her lips for him.

Myles tensed.

It was then she heard it.

His cell phone was ringing.

"Sorry. I have to get that." He let loose a deep breath and scooped up his phone. "Yeah?" he answered.

Roxxy stepped back from him to give him some privacy. She cleared the desk of the bloodied cloths and tossed them in the trash.

"Mac, I'm fine. Just a graze." He paused, apparently listening to whatever Sergeant MacArthur was saying—better yet, yelling.

Roxxy heard the deep rumble of Mac's voice clear across the small room.

How the hell did Mac know Myles was shot?

She walked toward the chair in front of the desk. Her feet were aching in her heels. Ending the day with a shoot-out in a fancy dress and high heels wasn't how she'd planned their evening.

The perfect ending to their night would have been her and Myles going back to the hotel to make love in the jacuzzi.

"Hold for now." Myles snagged her arm and brought her up against him.

She resisted at first.

He frowned and wrapped his forearm around her waist. "Do me a favor. Look into a Korey Norman."

Roxxy spun in his arms with a gasp. "I told you Korey wouldn't do something like this." She slapped a hand on his chest.

"Just do it, please?" Myles disconnected the call and slid the phone in his pocket. He pulled her to him and wrapped her up in his strong embrace. "I'm covering all bases. Mac will look into him. If he comes back clean, then he's off the suspect list."

"I know Korey. A killer is something he's not. He's an ass, but not a killer."

Myles studied her. Finally, he jerked his head into a nod. "Fine. But my gut is still telling me that they are coming for us."

"I was careful. No one followed us," she said.

"You did a good job making sure of that, but whoever that was, they waited for us. I don't want to let my guard down."

Roxxy rested her hands on his chest. "What do you need?"

"Guns. We need guns, something to protect us."

Roxxy grinned wide. "Well, Officer Burton." She turned on her southern charm. "You just so happen to be in the right place, suga."

20

"But before we do anything, I need to change my clothes," Roxxy declared, backing away from him.

He instantly missed having her curvy frame pressed against him.

But she was right.

She was still in her sexy black dress. There were some smudges on it from her sidewalk dash.

Myles wrestled with his shirt and put it back on, leaving it unbuttoned. His arm stung like hell, but there was no way he was going to let Roxxy know he was in pain.

"Let's be quick." He walked out of the office behind her and through the barn.

They jogged up the back stairs to the house. Roxxy opened the door and entered the home. Myles followed behind her, finding them in a kitchen that looked as if it belonged in a five-star restaurant.

"I'm sure my father is still up." Roxxy kicked her

shoes off and snagged them from the floor. She waved him behind her and disappeared down a hall.

They journeyed to the family room. Her father was sitting in an oversized plush recliner watching television. Earl's gaze swiveled to them as they entered.

"Wasn't expecting you two back so soon," Earl's deep voice broke the silence. He lifted a long-neck bottle to his lips and took a sip.

"Daddy, we have a problem," Roxxy announced.

Earl's hand paused, the mouth of the beer bottle resting on his lips before he pulled it away slowly.

His gaze hit Myles. He was instantly taken back to his basic training when he was a young, scrawny Myles and his sergeant stared him down.

"There was an altercation this evening," Myles began, stepping into the room.

"I heard there was a shoot-out in town. That was y'all?" Earl set his drink on the table beside him. He sat forward and rested his elbows on his knees.

"Unfortunately," Roxxy breathed.

"What happened?" Earl demanded.

Myles gave a quick recount of the events from the night, including their run-in with Korey and his gut feeling that they were being followed the entire night.

"The entire night? Even before we went to dinner?" Roxxy gasped. She spun on him. "Why didn't you say something?"

"I didn't want to ruin our night out. They hadn't made a move, so I wasn't sure what to expect." From the second they'd left the hotel, he'd felt eyes on them. She had already been paying close attention to him, and he hadn't wanted her to worry. They had been enjoying each other's company, and he'd hoped that whoever was observing them wouldn't have acted.

"Well, it was obvious you were expecting something, you had a gun on you!"

"As he should," Earl interrupted. The older man pushed off from his seat and stood to his full height. He strolled over to them.

Had it not been for the graying of his hair, Myles wouldn't have guessed the man would have a daughter Roxxy's age.

He placed an arm around Roxxy's shoulder and pressed a kiss to her forehead. "You are quite special, young lady, and I can't help but respect your young man for being prepared in this situation." Earl turned his attention to Myles.

He held his hand out to Myles who took the elder Sutton's hand in a firm grip.

"She means a lot to me, sir. I'll be damned if something was to happen to her," Myles admitted. It was the God's honest truth. He'd been pissed that the shooters had opened fire on them in public. He didn't care that he'd been hit. If something would have happened to his Roxxy, there'd be hell to pay.

"That's what I like to hear." Earl nodded to Myles.

"What do you like to hear?" Mrs. Sutton breezed into the room with a wide grin. Her smile instantly faded when she took one glance at the three of them. "What's going on?"

"I'm going to run upstairs and change my clothes. I'll be back in just a second." Roxxy brushed past them and disappeared.

"Looks like we need to head out to the shed, Momma," Earl proclaimed. He quickly brought Shelby up to date.

Her face remained void of all emotion as she listened to her husband.

Shelby casually strolled over to a small nook behind the couch and pulled a rifle out. She swung it up on her shoulder and flickered her gaze between Earl and Myles.

"No one shoots at my baby and gets away with it." She had a determined expression. The beautiful, middle-aged woman went from loving housewife to warrior in a blink of an eye.

This was one woman Myles wouldn't want to cross. The way she'd handled the gun let Myles know she was intimately familiar with it.

It was official.

Myles was hopelessly in love with not only Roxxy, but her family.

"I'm ready," Roxxy said from the doorway. She was no longer in her little sexy number. She was now in a black t-shirt, jeans, and sensible boots. Her hair was pulled back in a high ponytail, keeping the long tresses from her face.

Myles stalked across the room, unable to take his eyes off her. He pressed a hard kiss to her lips.

"Lead the way, Roxxy girl."

Myles followed Roxxy around the side of the barn. His gaze swept the area, landing on a small vegetable garden that was plush and well cared for. He could imagine Roxxy out here tending to it. Roxxy glanced over her shoulder at him and tossed him a sassy wink.

Earl and Shelby pulled up the rear. He didn't know where she was taking him, but watching her from behind, he knew he'd follow her anywhere.

They arrived at a storage shed a little way behind the barn, tucked into a thicket of trees.

"You, Officer Burton, are in for a treat," she announced. Roxxy took a key and inserted it into the lock. She pushed open the door and faced him.

"Ladies first." He waved to the dark space.

Roxxy and Shelby entered the building. A soft light lit up the room. The women disappeared from view.

"Burton," Earl called.

Myles turned to find the older man standing next to him. "Yes, sir?"

"Those two women in there mean the world to me." Earl's voice dropped low.

He stepped closer to Myles who didn't back away. Myles met the man's unwavering gaze.

"I want to know what trouble you are bringing to my land."

Myles sighed. "To be honest, sir, I'm not even sure. My sergeant had already gotten word and is looking into some leads for me."

"How the hell did he know already?"

"Hell if I know, but that's Mac for you." Myles brushed a palm over his head. Frustration filled him. He was used to running into the danger with guns blazing. It was a part of who he was. But now that he had someone who meant so much to him, fear crept up in the background. What if he couldn't keep her safe? "But I do know one thing. This ends today."

Earl nodded. "A lesson I took away from the Army was always trust your gut. If yours is saying those men are coming, then let's ready the welcome wagon."

Myles walked through the door and paused. Earl

shut it behind them before joining him. The room appeared like any other shed. Gardening tools hung on the walls, but Earl revealed a hidden door. Myles walked through it and was instantly impressed by the Sutton family.

Behind the makeshift storage area was a secured room with enough weapons and ammunition to outfit a small militia.

"Like what you see?" Roxxy grinned and spun around slowly with her hands up in the air.

Myles was unable to speak. He turned, taking in the shelves on the walls showcasing semiautomatic weapons, from rifles to handguns. There were even knives of all shapes and sizes on display. The respect he had for the Suttons skyrocketed.

"Beautiful," Myles murmured, his gaze landing on Roxxy.

"My dad and I have been collectors for years." Roxxy chuckled.

Myles stood by her, unable to decide where he wanted to start. Earl and Shelby moved around grabbing items. Myles felt like a kid in the candy store with limited funds.

"Some collection," he muttered. This was more than a regular family collection of weapons. His suspicions lay with Roxxy's father. There was more to Mr. Sutton than he let on.

"Let's just say, I've taken a few odd jobs here and there after I left the Army and the police force. Did some work for Department of Homeland Security and a few other branches that was off the books," Earl winked at Myles. "Had to pay the bills somehow until my company took off the ground."

Myles turned his attention to Roxxy in disbelief. "You, too?"

"Hell, no. I just love shooting things." She snickered, placing a Glock in a hip holster. She opened a set of double glass doors and pulled out a Kevlar vest. She slid it over her head, securing the straps at her waist. "And I'm damn good at it."

"Don't be shy now," Shelby said. She pointed to the wall in front of him. "Help yourself. Ammunition is located in the drawers below."

The room fell silent as they all prepared themselves. Myles glanced at Roxxy and felt the need to share his feelings with her, but now wasn't the best time with her parents standing around and her father having access to a countless amount of guns.

He'd wait until it was just the two of them.

He checked the small revolver and placed it in his empty holster on his ankle. He'd outfitted his body with a few weapons and was satisfied with what he'd chosen. His borrowed vest was comforting to him. It was a blatant reminder that this was not work. Someone was coming for him.

He was ready.

"What's the plan?" Roxxy asked. She leaned back against the table near her.

"Shelby is one hell of a long-range shooter," Earl volunteered.

"I'll post up in the barn," Shelby said. "It will give me a clear shot of the driveway."

"Earl and I will draw them away from the main area. Roxxy can stay back—"

"Like hell I will." Roxxy cut Myles off. She moved to stand before him. "Where you go, I go."

"Roxxy—"

"I got your six, Burton," Roxxy stared up at him with her wide eyes. She took his hand in hers and gave it a squeeze.

Those five words deflated any argument he would have been able to come up with.

"Fine," Myles murmured. He lifted her hand to his lips and pressed a kiss to the back of it. He was used to his men covering him. Be it his squad when he was in the Army or his SWAT teammates, but never the woman he loved. Hearing that she was willing to back him up almost brought him to his knees. Most men wanted a woman to cook and clean for them, but not Myles. He'd put his life on the line for others for his entire adult life, and to hear this little wisp of a woman had his back, meant everything.

"I'll draw them away from the house." Earl broke through Myles's thoughts. He turned to Shelby. "Make sure to cover me, Momma."

"I always do, honey."

21

The dark sky was cloudless with ample amount of stars lining the magnificent canvas. Roxxy glanced up and gazed at the moon. It was a beautiful sight to behold. She wished she could be lying down on a blanket with Myles without a care in the world.

Tonight would not be that night.

She made a promise to herself she'd get that perfect night with Myles.

Nature was a beauty, and she always wanted to make sure she took time to appreciate it.

The sounds of squeaky brakes filled the air off in the distance.

Roxxy tensed. She glanced at Myles who was staring off in that direction.

How the hell did he know someone would come?

It was late at night, and no one would be visiting at this time without calling ahead.

She and Myles were posted at the edge of the

woods near the driveway. They were able to see the house and the entire area around the front of it.

"Myles," she began.

He turned to her and rasied a finger to her lips.

"Not now, Roxxy," he murmured. He leaned down and pressed a quick kiss to her mouth. "When this is over, we need to have a long talk."

She nodded, unsure what that meant. A long talk?

The sound of tires slowly driving over gravel broke the silence. Roxxy tensed. She undid the holster at her side and took her Glock out. She was comforted by the weapon. Myles shifted to move in front of her. They were hidden by the thicket of trees. Only someone who was searching for them would see them.

"We can't let them get to the house," Myles whispered.

"Momma won't let that happen." Roxxy scoffed.

Her mother's shot was true, and whoever this was arriving, was about to learn.

They grew quiet at the sight of a dark sedan driving up to the edge of the drive. It braked to a halt. Roxxy squinted in the low light, trying to see more details of the car. She couldn't tell if it was the one from earlier, but it appeared to be the same color.

They watched in tense silence as the passenger doors and one of the back doors opened. Three men stepped from the vehicle. Each of them had guns in their hands.

Roxxy scanned the area, and the floor of her stomach dropped. She tapped Myles on the shoulder. Five men emerged from the woods on the side of the driveway. Where the hell had they come from?

Myles let out a soft growl.

"Take my phone," he whispered. He slipped it from his pants. "Take a picture of the plate and text it to Brodie. You'll find an old text from him."

"I'm not leaving—"

"Go," he snapped. He softened his words. "I need to figure out who the hell sent these people. That will hopefully give us a clue."

She paused before jerking her head in a nod. She slid the phone in her back pocket.

The men started walking up the driveway toward the house, staying close to the trees. An owl hooted off in the distance, drawing the men's attention. They stopped then pushed forward. Myles crept ahead slowly and disappeared into the darkness.

Roxxy cursed. She raised her weapon, not taking any chances of slipping, and headed toward the car. She arrived near the vehicle and didn't see anyone inside or around it. She wasn't sure why they'd brought a car into the driveway.

Getaway vehicle?

She swallowed hard. She replaced her gun back in the holster and pulled out Myles's phone. She ensured the flash was off. It would definitely alert the bad guys that they were on to them. She sent the picture off and peeked around the car.

It was quiet.

Too quiet.

Where the hell was her father?

Sliding Myles's phone into her pocket, she took the gun out and dipped back into the protection of the woods.

Roxxy tried to remain as quiet as she could as she made her way toward the direction Myles had vanished.

If they were coming for him, they were going to have to deal with her and her parents.

The men had spread out, disappearing into the woods. Myles had wondered if they were just going to walk right up the driveway to the house. When they ducked back into the shadows of the trees, it was exactly what Myles was hoping for. He had been trailing one of them unnoticed. They stopped at the end of the trees. Myles watched them and recognized they had a plan. This was no random hit. These men

248

had carefully laid-out plans and knew what they were looking for.

There was no way in hell he was going to allow these men to cause harm to the Suttons.

Myles bit back a growl. He remained hidden amongst the trees. He briefly shut his eyes, having to draw on his days when he was in the Army.

His eyes flickered open, and he had to beat down the rage that threatened to consume him. He crept behind the guy, who had let his guard down.

Myles flew into action. He wrapped an arm around his neck and clamped his other hand over his mouth to muffle his yell. Myles dragged him back deeper in the trees. He brought him upright and applied pressure to his neck with his forearm. Within seconds, the man's body became dead weight. Myles lowered him to the ground. He pulled out a few zip ties he'd taken from the Sutton's shed and secured the man's wrists.

Myles left him propped up against a tree and moved on.

He tried to will his heart to slow down.

He needed to be calm while he hunted.

Myles approached another one. He ducked behind a thick tree and looked around it at the perp. He had a radio that cut in with a person giving updates. It was on the lowest volume, but Myles heard the person.

"Lights are out in the house. They must be asleep."

Movement caught Myles's eye. He turned and saw another man walking toward the one with the radio. In a blink of an eye, he vanished. Myles froze. He relaxed once he saw a familiar figure.

Earl.

Looked like the older man still had it.

Two down. Six more to go.

"We move out, now," the one with the radio responded.

"Copy that."

Myles moved.

He took the man by surprise. Myles whipped him around and pulled back his arm. His fist slammed into the guy's face, sending him to the ground. The gun in his hands went flying somewhere in the brush. Myles released a curse.

"Myles Burton," the guy growled. He pushed off the ground. He reached up and wiped the blood from his face with the back of his hand. "We've been looking for you. Thanks for making our job easier."

"Who the hell are you people?" Myles demanded. "What the hell do you want?"

"Not for you to know. They just paid me."

He dove at Myles, who immediately blocked him. He swung a left uppercut that connected with the thug's stomach. Myles swung his right elbow down, connecting it with the back of his neck, rendering him unconscious. He fell forward, landing on the ground at Myles' feet.

Myles leaned down and searched him. He took the handheld radio and lowered the volume. He clipped it on to his belt buckle and bent down, running his hands over the man's body. He felt a bulge in the back pocket and took out a wallet. He took the driver's license out and put it back where he found it.

He secured this one like that last guy. He stood up straight, a stick breaking behind him. He whipped around, drawing the gun in his borrowed holster out.

"Jesus," Roxxy muttered. She had her weapon aimed at him. "It's me," she whispered, lowering her gun. She stepped forward, her gaze dropping to the guy on the ground.

Myles replaced the gun and waved her over to him.

"You good?" he asked.

"Yeah." She made her way to his side. "I found the other one you left back there. You're leaving a trail of bad guys. I could follow you anywhere."

"They're heading toward the house. They think I'm in there," he murmured.

She froze. "How do you know they are after you?"

"This one confirmed it before I knocked his ass out." Myles turned back toward the house. "We need to move. Now."

The sound of a distinct popping filled the air.

Gunfire.

"Momma," Roxxy exclaimed.

If Shelby was shooting, that meant the men were on the move to the house.

Myles unsheathed his weapon and held it up. He aimed it true as he walked out the edge of the trees. Just when he stepped from the hedges, a bullet whizzed by him and slammed into the tree nearest him. He pushed Roxxy back into the woods.

"Son of a bitch," Myles growled. "I want you in the house."

"No way." She shook her head. She raised her gun and rolled around the tree. She popped off a few shots and came back on the safe side. "Took two down."

Myles just stared at her. He'd never seen anyone appear so sexy before with a gun in their hands. He leaned forward and pressed a kiss to her lips. Her body molded to his. She broke away from him and stared up into his eyes.

"I love you," he blurted out.

He blinked.

Shit. Did he just say that in the middle of a shoot-out? What was wrong with him? He could have said it when they were alone, a romantic evening that included wine and—

"Oh, Myles." She reached up and cupped his jaw. "I love you, too."

A goofy smile spread across his face. Now that he'd said it, he didn't know what came next. This was new territory for him. He'd never thought he'd fall in love with someone, but here he was, head over heels in love with Roxxy Lynn Sutton.

"But, baby, we are going to have to finish this after the bullets stop firing." She patted him on his chest.

Where was his brain? Apparently on a vacation. Roxxy came around him, and he couldn't concentrate.

"Of course." The smile disappeared from his lips.

They had bad guys to stop.

He moved to the edge of the trees again and peeked out. The gunfire had quieted. He had one thing on his mind.

Protect Roxxy.

He'd be damned if she got hurt trying to protect him.

They needed to find out who these men were. Why would they target him? He'd made plenty of enemies over the years being a cop.

"We're going to make a run for the side of the house. We'll have a better position over there than we do here," Myles said. "I saw your father on the opposite side of the trees. I haven't seen him since."

"I'm sure Dad is fine. He's probably taken out all of the men over there and sitting down drinking a beer." She gave an unladylike grunt.

Well, Earl Sutton was definitely Myles's type of man.

"Are you ready?" he asked.

"Yeah, Mom will cover us."

They took off running out of the trees. Myles was in excellent shape, and he was impressed Roxxy was able to keep up with him. They arrived at the side of the house.

Myles pushed Roxxy behind him so he could look out around the corner, back at the woods.

The sounds of blades cutting through the air overhead drew his attention. He froze in place and glanced at the sky.

A black-and-white helicopter.

Myles grinned.

The cavalry was here.

Sirens off in the distance grew.

The helicopter circled around the roof of the home. It shined its spotlights down on the driveway and the woods surrounding the direct way before flying over to an open field.

"Friends?" Roxxy asked, cocking her beautifully sculpted eyebrow.

"The best. Let's go. Stay close to me."

With the threat of the police on their way, Myles was confident those men who weren't tied up, would run.

They skirted across the yard and headed toward the field where the helicopter had landed. The door opened, and out jumped Mac, Ash, Iker, and Brodie.

Each dressed in dark clothing and weapons on their body, they were a fierce-looking bunch.

"Just couldn't stay out of trouble, could you?" Ash asked, striding toward him.

Myles chuckled. "Am I glad to see you fuckers."

He met Ash for a firm friendly hug. His good friend gave him a hard squeeze before he released him.

"We heard you took fire earlier today." Mac didn't hold any punches and jumped straight to the point.

Myles's sergeant's focus locked on him.

"Here, too," Myles said grimly. He pulled Roxxy to his side. "Not sure why, but I was the target."

22

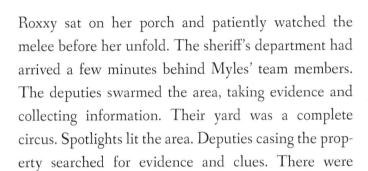

Roxxy sat on her porch and patiently watched the melee before her unfold. The sheriff's department had arrived a few minutes behind Myles' team members. The deputies swarmed the area, taking evidence and collecting information. Their yard was a complete circus. Spotlights lit the area. Deputies casing the property searched for evidence and clues. There were police cars, ambulances, and the paddy wagon parked on the grass in front of the house.

"You did good out there," Shelby murmured.

Roxxy jumped slightly, having not heard her mother approach.

Shelby sat next to her on the stairs.

"You did some fancy shooting yourself." Roxxy chuckled, glancing over at her mother.

Shelby Sutton was a force to be reckoned with. She appeared docile and sweet, but piss her off, and she'd unleash her wrath. It was Shelby who'd taught Roxxy to be strong and that she could still be a woman while brandishing her favorite gun. Their family collection was started and maintained by the lady of the Sutton family.

"Well, I had something to protect that means the world to me." Her mother patted her on the leg. "I was a little rusty at first, but it comes back to you."

Roxxy's gaze landed on her Myles speaking with his team and the sheriff. As if feeling her eyes on him, he turned and glanced in her direction. Their eyes met for a brief moment. His lips curled up into his crooked grin. Her heart stuttered at his look.

"He's a good man, Roxxy," Shelby said, obviously noticing the heated look between them.

Roxxy gazed down at her hands with a warm feeling spreading through her chest. She was rendered speechless. Her mother's assessment of Myles was spot on. He was one hell of a man.

He'd told her he loved her.

May not have been at the perfect time, but it was Myles. In the threat of danger, he let his true feelings be known to her. Had they not been getting shot at, she would have ripped his clothes off to show him how much she loved him.

"I know," she replied. She peered around. "Where's Dad?"

"He's over there speaking with Deputy Russel."

Her mother pointed over to the police van that housed the men Myles and her father had tied up.

The deputy patted her father on the back and gave a sharp nod. Roxxy was sure her father was giving him orders. Earl Sutton was well known in these parts. He was good friends with the sheriff, and when Earl spoke, they all listened.

Roxxy bit back a yawn. It was late, almost morning. She was ready to strip her clothes off, take a hot shower, and dive into her bed. She had a funny feeling it was going to be a long while before she'd be able to do either.

What she truly wanted was to do all of that and slide into a bed with Myles's arms wrapped around her.

Myles and his men strolled toward the house.

Her core clenched at the sight of her man. The clothes he'd worn to dinner were torn and tattered. He walked across the grass with an air of confidence. Protecting her and her family had been his top priority.

"Roxxy." Mac nodded to her. "Mrs. Sutton."

"Hello, Mac." Roxxy smiled. She waved to the other men standing behind him.

These men had somehow jumped a helicopter to come save a member of their team. It was obvious that the men were close and willing to do anything to help their brother when he was in danger.

"Sergeant MacArthur, welcome to my home. I wish it were under better circumstances." Shelby chortled. She stood and shook Mac's hand.

"That would have been nice. You all have a lovely piece of land." Mac gave a dry chuckle.

"Thank you." Her mother smiled. Shelby was always proud to show off the farm. "Can I offer you fellas something to drink? I made some iced tea this morning."

Roxxy's gaze landed on Myles who was motioning for her.

"Excuse me," she murmured. She stood and walked down the few steps to him.

"Come with me." He took her hand and guided her around the corner of the house.

"What's wrong?" She was uncertain why he needed to pull them away from everyone.

She leaned back against the house and waited. He palmed his bald head and stared at her.

"I meant what I said," he began. He appeared nervous which was rare for someone who was extremely confident and cocky. He stepped near her, closing the gap between them. "There's so much I want to say, but now isn't the time."

"I know." She sighed. She reached up and caressed his borrowed vest. "But that's okay, once they've all left—"

"That's the thing. I need to go with them," he interjected.

She paused her hand. "Oh."

"The sheriff is going to let us interview the men your father and I tied up. I have to know what is going on. This is more than what we know."

Roxxy nodded. She understood completely that he needed to finish whatever was started. He wouldn't be safe until they did. There would be no peace or rest until he'd solved this.

Hell, she wouldn't rest knowing someone was out there gunning for the man she loved. She leaned against him and took his hands in hers.

"I want you to go and get the answers we need." She lifted his hand to her lips and pressed a light kiss to the back of it. Those strong hands had given her so much pleasure. She rubbed her face against it. "Then I want you to come back to me and show me how much you love me."

Myles cupped her cheek and tilted her head back. He leaned forward and covered her lips with his.

"Roxxy, I'll be coming back for you."

Myles walked from the men's room at the sheriff's department in his newly borrowed clothing. One of the deputies had a pair of gray sweatpants and a sheriff's t-shirt in his locker that was slightly snug on Myles.

It would have to do for now. There hadn't been any time for him to run back to his hotel room and get a change of clothing. The clothes he had worn to dinner were ruined.

He walked through the small building toward where his teammates were standing. The sheriff was going to allow them to speak with the men who were apprehended. Myles couldn't wait to get into a room. He wanted the one who had shared the information about the men being paid to find him. They needed to continue their conversation.

He arrived in the small area to find Mac, Ash, Iker, and Brodie speaking quietly amongst themselves. They were waiting for the green light to interrogate the suspects.

"It's about time, lover boy," Ash joked.

Myles rolled his eyes and stopped next to his friend.

"So how did Roxxy love dining then a shoot-out?" Brodie snickered.

Ash and Iker chuckled with him.

"My girl likes shooting shit," Myles replied. He folded his arms in front of his chest. He winced slightly from the wound on his arm. Now that the adrenaline had worn off, he was feeling the pain.

"You need to get that checked out." Mac nodded to his shoulder.

"I'm fine." Myles shook his head.

"I'm not suggesting. That's an order." Mac narrowed his gaze on Myles.

He blew out a deep breath. He didn't want to argue with his sergeant. Mac was like a pit bull, and when he set his sights on something, he didn't give up.

"Fine, but after we're done here. I have things to do." Roxxy's face came to mind. He hadn't wanted to leave her, but he had to be involved in the interrogation. Men came gunning for him, he needed to find out why. Roxxy was almost certain the shooting after they'd left the ice cream parlor had nothing to do with her ex, but he wanted to rule everyone out before accepting her reasoning. "What did you find out on Korey Norman?"

"Nothing worth anything," Brodie answered. He was a whiz when it came to technology. "Stand-up guy, pays his taxes, decent hard worker. Just an average American citizen who don't know how to keep his dick in his pants."

Myles's gaze cut to him. "What?"

"It's amazing what you find on social media. So apparently the idiot cheated on Roxxy with some waitress. The same woman has now posted all over his social media that he's been cheating on her with some other chick." Brodie chuckled.

Myles shook his head. Korey had fucked up, and now Myles was reaping all of the rewards.

"I want in on the interrogation." Myles turned to Mac. Usually he stayed out of this type of thing. Mac, Declan, and Ash were usually the go-to when it came to getting information out of the bad guys.

But this was personal.

It had been him they were looking for.

Mac paused and stared at him for a second before jerking his head in a nod. "We can tag team. I'm not sure how much time the sheriff is going to give us, so its best if we go in with each other."

"We missed out on all the fun," Ash said. "It's been a few days since I've had to fire my weapon."

"You don't need any extra action. Deanna would kill us if you were harmed." Myles laughed. "I'm shocked you're even here. Baby is due soon. You should be sticking close to home."

"True, but when I hear my friend and brother came under fire while out to dinner with his woman, there's no way I could stay away." Ash turned serious.

Myles nodded, understanding what his friend was saying. They had a bond. The entire SWAT team was close. Myles was actually surprised that everyone didn't show up.

"No way was I getting left behind." Iker clapped him on the back.

"Where did y'all get a helicopter from?" Myles asked. He scratched his head, still in shock that his team had shown up in a borrowed bird.

"Don't worry your pretty bald head about that. You know I know people." Brodie chuckled.

Myles stared at him for a brief moment then shook his head. Brodie had too many contacts with resources he never understood.

"Sergeant MacArthur?" Sheriff Anderson walked toward them from the area where the suspects were being held. He stopped near their group, clutching some paperwork in his hand. "Sorry it took so long. Been a while since we had to process so many people."

"Not a problem, Sheriff. We're patient men," Mac replied.

"Now I can't let you in there for long, but seeing how they were on Sutton property, I'll bend the rules." The sheriff took his hat off and burrowed his hand into his hair. "The Suttons are a good family and close friends of mine, so whatever you can find out to help you, by all means, go ahead."

Myles was running on fumes at the moment, and sleep was a long way away. As soon as he could, he was leaving to go back to Roxxy. He was head over heels in love with her. If he hadn't learned anything else watching his friends fall in love, he'd learned that he needed to scoop up the woman he loved and hold on to her. Tomorrow wasn't promised, and he needed to use every day he had to show Roxxy how much he loved her.

"We appreciate it, Sheriff." Mac nodded.

"Here's what we have so far on the men. None of them are from around these parts." Anderson handed the papers to Mac.

Myles moved closer to Mac so he could get a good look at them. The papers were the men's rap sheets with their pictures on them. Mac shifted through them.

"That one." Myles pointed to the sheet on top. It was the thug from the woods who'd confirmed they were after him. "I want in on him."

"Brodie, you and Iker will go have a chat with these two. Myles and I will take these two," Mac announced. He handed two of the rap sheets to Brodie while he passed the other one to Myles.

"Follow me. I have two already in separate rooms waiting. When you want the other two, we'll bring them out of the holding area." Anderson motioned for them to follow him.

Myles walked behind Mac, his gaze glued to the paper in his hand.

Whit Green was the thug's name. His sheet was as long as Myles was tall.

Myles froze and released a curse.

He looked up and found all eyes on him.

"What is it?" Mac asked.

"Let me see the other sheets."

Brodie handed them to him. He shuffled through them all and instantly picked up a common associate between them all.

Known affiliations: Demon Lords.

"All of them belong to the Demon Lords," he said. His gaze met Mac's.

Someone released a curse. The Columbia SWAT team had bad blood between the infamous gang.

"So they are going after members of SWAT?" Iker narrowed his eyes and folded his arms in front of him.

"Well, they know we won't back down from them," Brodie replied.

"We go in and find out who wanted Myles dead. Let's get them talking," Mac instructed.

They all nodded.

"Then when we're done in here, Brodie, I want you to find out everything you can about these men. I want to know what they take in their coffee and anything else you can find."

Myles handed the papers back to Brodie.

He was ready to go in the room and find out what the hell these people wanted.

If they were after him because he was SWAT, the Demon Lords would feel their wrath again.

"Let's go." Myles brushed past his teammates and headed in the direction the sheriff had disappeared.

They arrived at the interrogation rooms. The sheriff updated them on which men were in the room. First up was Whit Green.

"Remember we want him talking," Mac said. He moved next to Myles.

"I know. He already gave me enough information earlier," Myles bit out. He had to keep his cool. Beating the man to within an inch of his life wasn't going to get him anywhere but jail himself. Myles blew out a deep breath.

"You good?" Mac arched an eyebrow at him.

"Yeah. Don't kick his ass. Got it."

Mac chuckled and opened the door. It was a small room with a table, three chairs, and a two-way mirror. Standard procedure called for the room to be recorded.

"Good morning." Mac pulled up a chair in front of Whit.

Whit sat at the table with his head resting on the surface and hands cuffed in front of him. He slowly lifted when Myles shut the door. He glanced at Mac and Myles and smirked.

"So they sent the good ol' boys in here to rough me up?" Whit gave a dry snicker.

"That would be illegal," Mac replied drolly.

"Like that would stop ya," Whit taunted.

"You sure didn't have a problem gunning for me," Myles growled. He narrowed his eyes on the man, taking in all his features.

"I was lost." Whit grinned. "Didn't know where I was. Me and my buddies were hunting."

Myles had to push down the urge to punch Whit in the face. He was quickly trying Myles's patience.

"Hunting? That's your excuse?" Mac took a seat in the chair across from Whit.

He acted cool and aloof, but Myles knew his sergeant, and Mac was anything but. He was a bulldog and had a bite that was just as vicious.

"This is South Carolina. Us country boys like to hunt."

"But you're not from around here." Myles leaned back against the wall. He glared at the suspect.

Whit was lying. Both he and Mac knew it.

"There ain't no law that says I can't travel around the state."

"There's a law against hunting down someone. A police officer." Mac rested his forearms on the table. "You think we're just going to let that go?"

Whit leaned back as far as the handcuffs would allow. "So is this where you play bad cop, good cop to try to get information out of me?"

"Bad cop, good cop is shit you see on television." Myles huffed. Where did this guy think he was? In a movie? That routine was common in television shows and movies. They didn't play games like that when interrogating suspects. "How about you tell us why you were after me. You said it yourself in the woods."

"I didn't say shit," Whit denied.

Myles glared at him. "Excuse me?"

"After you knocked me out, I don't remember nothing. I think I should sue your department. I'm sure I'll get plenty of—"

Myles pushed off the wall and stalked toward the table. "You son of a bit—"

"Stand down, Burton," Mac barked. He glanced at Myles and held up a hand. He turned back to Whit, his voice dropping low. "Look, we know you're associated with the Demon Lords. They don't have a good history with our squad. You want to go down with them, fine, but I will tell you they don't protect their own."

Mac stood from his chair.

"What the fuck is that supposed to mean? Demon Lords protect their own," Whit snapped.

"Not sure when you joined, but you should—"

"You think the Demon Lords are after you?" Whit turned his attention to Myles. "Naw, they don't give a shit about you. But you need to watch your back. You cops say you stand behind each other, but I know from firsthand experience y'all can be just as crooked as criminals."

"What the hell is that supposed to mean?" Myles placed his hands on the table.

"The guy who hired us was a cop." Whit snickered.

"Why should we believe you?" Mac folded his arms in front of his chest.

"He didn't have a badge on or anything, but I know a cop when I see one." Whit sniffed. "Y'all walk around like your shit don't stink, like you're above everyone. That dude was a cop, no question."

Myles stood stall and glanced at Mac.

Shit.

This was fucked up.

"Now that I told you that information, cut me a deal." Whit chuckled. "Ain't that what cops do for information?"

"What information? I don't remember nothing." Myles turned and stalked out of the room. He ignored the shouts from the prisoner.

It was official. There was not only a mole in the department, but a traitor.

He and his men would find out who it was.

They'd make that person pay.

23

"You have got to be shitting me." Iker shook his head. "I mean, we all kept mentioning it, but this puts the nail in the coffin."

They all stood outside the sheriff's building. Myles remained silent while his team discussed what Whit had shared with him and Mac.

"We didn't get any good information out of the others," Brodie said. "They didn't know nothing."

"So they're about to go to jail for shit they didn't understand." Ash snickered. "Where do they find these guys at?"

"But who would want you dead?" Mac asked.

Myles shook his head. He'd had run-ins with plenty of people. He could think of one cop who didn't care for him, but he doubted that it went so deep as to put a hit out on him.

"The only person I can think of is Reeves." Myles shrugged.

"He wouldn't have the balls," Iker grumbled.

"What are you talking about? He wouldn't stand a chance against Myles. A coward would hire someone to take someone out," Brodie said.

"He's right, but come on. Reeves was pissed at Myles because he felt his chance was blown for SWAT. Is that serious enough to kill him?" Ash looked around at them.

The group fell quiet for a minute.

"Brodie, I want reports on my desk with everything you can find on these men. We need to find out who hired them. Who has a connection with the Demon Lords to put out a hit on Myles." Mac's voice was low.

"As soon as I get back home to my computer, I'll find everything. I can only do so much on my phone." Brodie nodded. He would, too. Brodie had a way about computers. If it was uploaded on the internet somewhere, he could find it. He was one dangerous man. "Don't worry. We're going to get to the bottom of this."

"When we return, we're all going to meet. Not at the station. Somewhere safe," Mac said.

Nods went around. Apparently speaking at the station wasn't safe. Iker was right. They all assumed and had strong suspicions that there was someone leaking information about SWAT to the notorious gang. The SWAT team had been instrumental in causing chaos within the illegal organization.

It was time for them to find the mole.

This person evidently wanted Myles dead.

There was no telling what else this person had done.

"We should head back now," Iker said. A yawn overtook him. He shook his head. "I'm beat. I need about a good ten hours of sleep."

Myles was running on adrenaline at the moment. He hadn't slept in over twenty-four hours and he would pay for it. But right now, he had something— someone—on his mind.

Roxxy.

He had to go to her.

They had unfinished business.

"Hey, I'm going to take an extra day," Myles announced.

Mac nodded while the guys snickered.

"Thee mighty hath fallen," Ash murmured.

Myles glared at his friend. He remembered the day Ash told him about Deana. His friend was pussy-whipped before he'd touched the woman. It took him almost a year to approach Deana.

"I just want to make sure Roxxy and her family are good," he said.

"Roxxy is a special woman," Mac began. He slapped Myles on the back. "She's good for you."

"Any woman who can handle a gun like her is a gem. She got a sister?" Iker rubbed his chin.

Chuckles went around.

"Well, when you return, we're going to meet. My house. I'll bring the food, y'all bring the booze," Mac said.

"Sounds like a plan." Brodie nodded.

"Let's return home, boys." Mac turned to Myles. "Call me when you get back into town."

"Will do."

Roxxy rolled over in her bed. It had taken her a while to drift off to sleep after the night they'd had. By the time the police had all left her family's property, it was damn near seven in the morning. She snuggled down into her blankets farther. She didn't have to work today. That was the one good thing about being the boss's daughter, she could make her own schedule. She could work from anywhere. She just had to go out on the audits.

She wasn't sure what time it was. The house was quiet. She was sure her parents were already up and moving around. Nothing stunned Earl and Shelby Sutton. She was so proud of how her parents and Myles had worked to protect their property.

It did bother her to learn those men had been hunting down Myles.

As much as she hated Korey, she knew he wasn't behind that. It wasn't in him. He was an ass, but he wasn't a killer.

There was a slight tap at her door.

"Come in." She sighed. She just wanted another hour of sleep, then she'd get up and join the world.

"Were you sleeping?" a familiar deep voice said from behind her.

Roxxy flew to a sitting position and faced the newcomer.

"Myles?" she whispered. She had thought he would have taken off and gone back to Columbia. She understood his job and finding out who was gunning for him was important. Her eyes greedily took him in. He must have had to borrow clothes from the sheriff's department, and she did have to say she would need to thank whoever lent him the sweatpants. "What are you doing here?"

"You didn't think I would leave without seeing you, did you?" He moved across the room. He sat on the edge of her bed and reached for her hand. He brought it up to his mouth and laid a kiss on the back of it.

"I'm sure you have work stuff to handle." She shrugged.

"But that doesn't come before you."

Her breath caught in her throat.

"I meant what I said in the woods. I know it wasn't the best time, but it was how I feel about you, and not knowing what we faced, I wanted to tell you." His dark eyes bored into her.

There was nothing but honestly in the deep pools. Something she knew he would always share with her. Unlike with Korey, she would never have to question whether or not he was telling the truth. Myles was a man of his word and very trustworthy. He'd certainly earned the trust of her parents.

She smiled. She didn't need a deep expression of love like in the movies.

It had been perfect.

"Same here," she whispered. She slid closer to him. She didn't know what she looked like but she didn't care. They way Myles watched her had her feeling like the most beautiful woman in the world.

"So what are we going to do about it?" he asked.

His teasing gaze made her smile grow wider.

"Oh, I don't know. Maybe we should take it a day at a time."

"I was thinking of consummating our love now," he growled playfully. He stood and kicked off his shoes.

"What?" She laughed watching him lie on the bed. "Myles, my parents!"

He pulled her to him. She wasn't going to struggle

too hard. Roxxy was right where she wanted to be. She snuggled next to him, breathing in his scent. Her head rested on his firm chest.

"Earl and Shelby were leaving as I was coming." He chuckled. "They told me to go wake you."

"Really?" She tilted her head back to look him in the eyes. "And if I would have been asleep when you came to my room, what would you have done?"

"Maybe start off with a kiss." He leaned down and pressed a hard kiss to her lips.

She released a groan.

She needed more.

"So how long do I have you?" she asked breathlessly.

"Well, physically, another twenty-four hours." He paused and stared into her eyes. "I do have to go back to Columbia. There's some shit about to go down, and I need to be there."

"That's okay," she breathed. She understood. As angry as she was for those men attacking them, she wanted Myles to find who'd done this. There would be no way they could relax while someone was out there sending men for him. Looking over his shoulder for his entire life wasn't worth it. "Find the person who did this. I'm not going anywhere."

Myles paused, his gaze raking over her. She meant every word. She was in love with him and would wait for him. Myles reached up and ran a tender finger along her face. He cupped her cheek. She leaned into his warm palm, turned her head, and pressed a kiss on it.

"Roxxy Sutton." His voice grew thick with emotion. "I love you."

"I love you, too, Myles Burton."

He covered her mouth with his. It was gentle, loving and sensual all rolled up in one. She wrapped her arms around his neck. The kiss grew deeper. Myles pushed her backwards where she landed on her back. He rolled over her, bracing himself above her. They pushed the blankets out of the way, allowing him to settle down into the valley of her thighs. She welcomed his weight. There was nothing better than the feel of her man on her.

"How much?"

"Did my parents say where they were going?" She arched an eyebrow. If she knew Earl and Shelby, they would be gone for a while.

"They said something about the market." Myles left a string of kisses on her jaw before nuzzling her neck.

Market? They'd be gone for hours.

She had enough time for what she had in mind to show Myles how much she loved him.

"Clothes off, Officer Burton," she ordered. She

snagged the edge of his shirt. She tugged it up and over his head. His strong, muscular chest came into view. She slid her hands across his back and practically purred from the feeling of his skin underneath her palms.

He gave a brief chuckle. "Anything for you, Roxxy."

EPILOGUE

"Sarena, Aspen, and Deana, I'd like you to meet my girl, Roxxy," Myles said, introducing Roxxy to the girls.

They all grinned at him before turning their attention to Roxxy.

He and Roxxy had arrived slightly late for the gathering. It had only taken them a week of a long-distance relationship to decide they didn't want to be so far apart from each other. Roxxy had started moving her things to his place. It hadn't taken much coaxing from him to talk her into moving to Columbia. Her parents had given their blessing, and Roxxy had packed up her car and moved half of her things already.

This was all new territory for Myles, but he couldn't see himself with anyone but Roxxy.

He needed her close to him.

She was his other half.

She would still be able to work for her father's company while living in Columbia.

Everything was perfect.

"It's such a pleasure to meet you." Sarena stepped forward with her hand outstretched.

"Thank you for having me. You have a beautiful home." Roxxy smiled while she shook Mac's wife's hand.

"We finally get to meet the woman who captured Myles. You dear, are a unicorn." Deana laughed. She pulled Roxxy into a hug.

Myles chuckled, shaking his head. He hadn't been that bad. Deana gave him a wink over Roxxy's shoulder.

She approved.

The way the women moved around Roxxy and immediately started talking and asking questions led him to believe she'd fit in the group just fine. They had forgotten about him that fast.

"Yo, Myles, you staying in here with the women?" Zain asked from the doorway.

"Be right there," he called out. He tugged on Roxxy's hand to get her attention. "I'll be down in the family room if you need me."

"She won't," Aspen joked. They shooed him toward the door. "From what I hear, you are good with guns. You think you could take us to the gun range?"

Roxxy lit up with that question. "Girl, of course I

can. I've been handling a weapon the same amount of time I've been walking this earth."

Myles didn't know why he had been worried she'd mesh with the girls. He left the room, going to meet up with his team. This wasn't their usual social visit.

Brodie was to report back his findings tonight.

Myles headed to the family room where he found the guys lounging around.

"It's about time. We thought you'd be staying in the kitchen." Iker snickered.

"Shut up. I wanted to do a proper introduction." Myles rolled his eyes. What was he supposed to do? Let Roxxy roam the house and not introduce her to anyone?

"She's fine. The girls will welcome her." Ash tossed him a cold beer.

He caught it with one hand and took a seat next to Declan.

"I'm sure the girls are asking her ten million questions." Declan chuckled. He took a sip of his drink. "The girls will have her added in their clique in no time."

It was amazing how quickly the women had bonded. They had become the best of friends.

"Okay, now that everyone is here, I just want to make an announcement before we hear from Brodie." Mac grabbed the television remote and turned it on.

Brodie stood from the wet bar and took the remote from Mac. "I want to use your television to show something," he muttered. He changed the channel and turned back to his computer. "Go ahead and start while I get this up and running."

"Officer Knight has accepted the position of SWAT," Mac announced.

Clapping went around the room.

Knight was a solid cop. She would make a great addition to the team. Everyone had nothing but good things to say about her.

"She'll start training with us next week," Declan chimed in. "I want everyone on their best behavior."

"We will welcome her with open arms, like we do everyone when they join us." Ash held up his beer.

"Hear, hear." They all raised their beers in the honor of the new addition to the team.

The television screen turned blue, capturing everyone's attention.

"All right, men. The information you have all been waiting for." Brodie typed out a few commands on his computer.

The television showed photographs of the four men Myles and Earl had captured on the Sutton farm.

Myles took a long pull from his drink.

"I did as Mac asked and I ran a check on all of them. When I say I flipped them inside out, I can now tell you who they had a crush on in the third grade, what brand of underwear they prefer, and how often they shit."

"Yeah, I don't need to know that," Zain muttered.

"Me neither." Iker chuckled.

"Go ahead, Brodie. What did you find?" Mac asked.

"Thank you, Sergeant," Brodie eyed the room.

Even Myles had to roll his eyes. They all wanted to hear what he'd found with his research.

"Anywho, I linked them all together; it all goes back to the Demon Lords which we knew. The Demon Lords haven't quite bounced back from the last time we hit them hard. There's been some power struggles, some parts of the gangs branching out on their own while even some are doing for-profit jobs on the side. This is where the bandit of men that was captured came into play."

The room fell quiet while Brodie spoke.

"They've been taking odd jobs here and there and are all wanted on multiple charges. South Carolina and Georgia are going to have a nice little fight. They are wanted in both states. So I had to dig deep to try to trace who the person was that hired them. Of course, I ran their bank statements and didn't find any deposited checks. That would have been too easy."

Myles was impressed by the information Brodie had found so far.

"Any validation to what the suspect said? He's accusing a cop of taking out a hit on another cop," Ash said. "How many times have we gone up against this gang? He could just be saying that to put blue against blue."

"I wish I could say that he was lying, but I have reason to believe Whit was telling the truth." Brodie hit another command on his phone. "I ran their phone records and went through their text messages and found one message to Whit from a burner phone setting a meeting. I checked the address, and it was a small library."

"Shit, this is intense work, Brodie. Good job," Declan murmured.

"Thanks. Now this part wasn't hard at all. I had the address of the library and date, so I hacked into their security cameras. This is where they made their mistake. They met during broad daylight where security cameras can easily capture your face." He hit a button on the keyboard, and a grainy picture came up.

Myles squinted and froze.

He recognized the man in the picture with Whit.

"Son of a bitch," someone murmured.

"Hey, guys!" Sarena called out, walking in the room.

Aspen, Deana, and Roxxy filed in behind her.

Roxxy had a wide grin on her face. She was practically radiating. She slid onto his lap and gave him a small kiss.

"I missed you," she murmured.

He automatically wrapped an arm around her and pulled her closer. Each woman was next to their men, snuggled up close to them.

"Not as much as I missed you." He pressed another kiss to hers.

"Did y'all have a breakthrough?" Her gaze landed on the television screen.

He tightened his hold on her and brought her back where he could rest his chin on her shoulder.

"Yeah, this is big. You love me, right?" he asked.

"You know I do." She sighed.

"Well, the road is about to get bumpy." He glanced back at the screen.

The room was silent while everyone apparently had to process what they were looking at on the screen.

Roxxy turned on his lap and placed her arm around his neck.

"As long as we're together, I'm ready for anything."

THE END

Want more romantic suspense from Peyton Banks? Check out her Trust and Honor series now!

Click Here!

A NOTE FROM THE AUTHOR

Dear reader,

Thank you for taking the time to read Dirty Alliance. I hope you enjoyed Myles and Roxxy's story! If you loved it, then please leave a short review on the platform you purchased this book on.

It doesn't matter how long or how short, all reviews matter.
I know a lot of you are wondering who is next and I will share it here with you! Brodie will be featured in Dirty Justice (Special Weapons & Tactics 5)!

Warm wishes,
Peyton Banks

DALLAS (TRUST & HONOR 1)

Black with four sugars.

That was how he liked his coffee.

Candi bit her lip to keep from smiling. While waiting for the coffee machine to finish brewing, she grabbed a tall paper traveling cup and counted out the sugars.

The kitchen was bustling with the cooks scurrying around getting ready for the dinner rush. Glancing at her watch, Candi knew he would be arriving for his shift any minute.

"How is it someone like him is sweet on you but gruff with everyone else?"

Candi spun slightly to see her friend and coworker, Kay, arrive at her side. Kay Moran was downright gorgeous. Tall, thin, with thick blonde hair, she turned the head of any man with a pulse. When Candi had been hired as a server, the two of them had hit it off and became fast friends.

Candi rolled her eyes at Kay's raised eyebrows. Kay didn't have to say what she was thinking. Candi read her loud and clear.

"I don't know." Candi shrugged. She rotated back to the coffeemaker to find it had finished brewing. "I keep the coffee coming. You should try being nice sometime. You can always win over a bear with honey."

Her lips spread into a silly grin. Bear didn't even begin to describe him.

Dallas McNeil.

Just the sound of his name had her wanting to sigh and daydream about the tall, muscular bouncer. Her heart fluttered with the thought of seeing him. Her core always clenched with need at his intense gaze.

"Yeah, and he'll bite my damn arm off if I tried," Kay muttered.

Candi chuckled and poured Dallas a hefty cup of java. "He's not that bad."

She couldn't keep the grin from spreading wider. She met Kay's gaze and laughed.

Dallas was a bit rough around the edges, but he was protective of her. All the bouncers who worked in the bar ensured the females were safe, but Dallas went a little above and beyond his duty.

The little hole-in-the-wall, The Commoner was

located in Downtown Las Vegas, and the place could get rowdy. Candi had perfected dodging wandering hands, but once in a while one connected with her ample bottom.

That was when Dallas stepped in.

The servers were not to be touched in any way. The bar and grill wasn't that type of place. In Nevada, there were plenty of establishments where men could get anything they wanted from a woman, but The Commoner was not one of them.

The Downtown Las Vegas scene was up-and-coming, with numerous bars and restaurants within walking distance that attracted the tourists away from the strip. The draw was the good food, drinks, and fun atmosphere that kept the bars packed. The Commoner was a popular pub, and the tips were great.

"Well, he certainly has his eye on you." Kay gently shoved her with her elbow.

"Whatever," Candi muttered, busying herself by putting the top on the cup. Deep down inside, she knew she had a crush on Dallas, but she didn't think she could act on it. She had too much baggage and couldn't ask a man to take any of it on.

Dallas was a good guy. He moonlighted at The Commoner, but he worked full time for the Las Vegas police department. She'd heard some talk that he had been in the service which she could totally see by his demeanor.

"Don't act like you don't know it." Kay pushed off the counter and walked past her toward the door that led out to the main room.

"I'm just taking a cup of coffee to my coworker." Candi snorted. Her heart raced with the thought of seeing Dallas tonight. She smoothed down her long, dark hair and wiped her hands on her jeans.

"You look beautiful, as usual." Kay smirked.

Candi ignored her friend and tried to will her heart to slow down.

She grabbed the cup and followed Kay out the door into the main area of the bar. The light was low, and the place was already filling up with customers. She only had a few minutes until her shift started. By the looks of it, she may be jumping in a little early.

Her gaze roamed the dark interior before landing on the familiar figure.

Everything faded away.

She had eyes only for him.

Gripping the cup tight, she separated from Kay and headed in his direction. Her breaths came fast as she took him in. Like the other bouncers, he wore a black shirt that had the word 'security' on the front. His biceps were on display when the short sleeves of the shirt slipped up.

Candi drank in the tattoos that lined his arms. She would give her left boob to be able to study them up close and personal.

His dark jeans hugged him perfectly. As if feeling her eyes on him, he turned away from the other bouncer, Tanner. His intense gaze slowly perused her body, and her breath escaped her.

She ignored the scream of her lungs. Her hips swayed a little more, she held in her tummy—not wanting to show off her slight pudge as much—and kept walking toward him.

Breathe! a voice screamed.

She inhaled deeply, and a slight shyness overcame her. What was her problem?

Biting her lip, she refused to look away. She was playing with fire. She wasn't ready for anything with a man, but there was something about Dallas.

He was certainly different from her ex-husband. Just the thought of Lamont had her blinking, snapping her out of the trance Dallas wove over her. It was like having a cold splash of water being thrown on her. Her step faltered slightly, but she kept going.

What was it about men and their muscles that just drew her to them like a moth to a flame?

But Dallas was nothing like Lamont.

In her gut, she knew that.

Lamont was controlling. Liked to use his fists to

show her he was more powerful than her. That he could make her do what he wanted with his fist.

But no more.

She'd finally got the nerve to leave.

It had taken a while, but she had done it.

The last time Lamont had put his hands on her, she'd ended up in the hospital with a broken arm.

That had been the final straw.

The nurses in the emergency room had been sympathetic and had stayed with her until the police had arrived. She had lost touch with who she was, and a reflection of herself in the bathroom at the hospital had changed everything. The person staring at back at her was a stranger.

She was tired of living her life in fear. Afraid that one small thing would set Lamont off. Scared that one day she'd be brought to the hospital in a body bag.

That night, her life had transformed.

She would take back control. One step at a time.

When the female police officer had approached her, Candi didn't wait for her to ask questions.

"I want to press charges," she'd whispered.

The woman had nodded and asked her the vital information she'd needed.

Snapping out of the past, Candi arrived at Dallas's side, and all of the fear and worry she'd harbored just dissipated.

His dark stare took her breath away. His gaze dropped down to the cup in her hands, and his lips tilted up ever so slightly.

Her fear was completely gone.

Dallas was different.

"Hey, Dallas," she murmured. She held the cup up to him.

He reached out and took it from her. Their fingers faintly brushed each other. She lingered for a brief second then pulled her hand back.

"Just the way you like it."

"Thanks, Candi." He took a sip of it, and his eyes fluttered shut for a second before opening again.

Her heart quivered at the look of contentment on his face.

"It's perfect."

"Where's my coffee?" Tanner asked. He feigned as if he was hurt, clutching his chest.

"It's still in the kitchen. You can go grab it when you want." She playfully shrugged her shoulder. It wasn't Tanner who had captured her eye. He was a nice guy and moonlighted at The Commoner like Dallas. He was handsome and always had women visiting the bar hanging off him.

"That's just wrong. Dallas is the meanest son of a—"

"Watch it, Tanner," Dallas's deep voice rumbled, cutting Tanner off.

It washed over her in waves and sent goosebumps down her arms. His gaze cut to Tanner, who held up his hands in defeat.

"Did you work today?" she asked.

He nodded, taking another sip of the coffee. She made a mental note to keep it coming for him. He wasn't a man of many words that she was aware of. He was more the silent, brooding type who dripped sex appeal.

"Candi!" a voice called out behind her.

She glanced over her shoulder. Her boss, Adam, waved her down.

"I guess duty calls," she said, turning toward to Dallas and Tanner. She backed away and spun on her heel before she said something crazy.

Like ask Dallas out for coffee or something when the bar closed.

Walking toward Adam, she could feel Dallas's gaze on her. Well, if he was going to watch her, she'd put on a show. She swung her wide hips and flipped her hair over her shoulder.

"Hey, can you clock in now?" Adam asked once she stopped in front of him. He was already looking frazzled, and the night had barely begun.

"Sure. I don't mind," she said.

"You'll take your normal area. Tina called off, and I'm going to try to see if Kate can come in." He patted her on her shoulder while walking away.

She glanced back to Dallas and met his gaze from across the room. Her lips curved up in a small smile. She quickly made her way to the bar and grabbed her apron from behind it.

"Looks like it's going to be a busy night," Tony, the bartender, said.

"Hey, Tony. Guess so. That means good tips." She laughed, tying the ties of her apron around her. She took straws and stuffed them in the front pockets, preparing herself.

"It better be. Daddy got bills to pay." He laughed, too, wiping the counter down. The bar only had a few seats open. The patrons' attention was on the basketball game.

"Don't we all." She snickered. Grabbing a pen, she headed out into the busy atmosphere and walked toward the table that Jenny, the hostess, had just seated.

The familiar sensation of being watched filled her. She glanced over toward where Dallas stayed posted and met his gaze. He didn't act like he was looking anywhere else. He nodded to her, and she knew they were going to have a good night.

"Hi, I'm Candi," she greeted the couple at the table with a smile.

With Dallas there, she'd have no worries.

Want to read more from Peyton's book, Dallas? Download it now!

Click HERE to snag the first book in the Trust & Honor series!

ABOUT THE AUTHOR

Peyton Banks is the alter ego of a city girl who is a romantic at heart. Her mornings consist of coffee and daydreaming up the next steamy romance book ideas. She loves spinning romantic tales of hot alpha males and the women they love. Make sure you check her out!

Sign up for Peyton's Newsletter to find out the latest releases, giveaways and news! Click HERE to sign up!

Want to know the latest about Peyton Banks? Follow her online

ALSO BY PEYTON BANKS

Current Free Short Story

Summer Escape

Special Weapons & Tactics Series

Dirty Tactics (Special Weapons & Tactics 1)

Dirty Ballistics (Special Weapons & Tactics 2)

Dirty Operations (Special Weapons & Tactics 3)

Dirty Alliance (Special Weapons & Tactics 4)

Dirty Justice (Special Weapons & Tactics 5) TBD

Trust & Honor Series (BWWM)

Dallas

Dalton (Coming soon)

Interracial Romances (BWWM)

Pieces of Me

Hard Love

Retain Me

Emerging Temptation: A BWWM Romance Limited
Edition Collection

Tempt Me: A Romance Limited Edition Collection
(Charity Anthology coming soon)

Mafia Romance Series

Unexpected Allies (The Tokhan Bratva 1)

Unexpected Chaos (The Tokhan Bratva 2) TBD

Unexpected Hero (The Tokhan Bratva 3) TBD

Made in the USA
Columbia, SC
15 March 2025